SALTWATER SWEETS

SHELL COVE BOOK 3

MEREDITH SUMMERS

CHAPTER 1

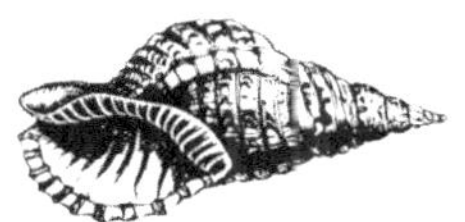

Gina Gallagher couldn't believe that her future happiness hinged solely on tracking down her cheating, embezzling louse of a husband.

Not that she wanted to see him, far from it. What she *did* want was her portion of their life savings, which he'd stolen after emptying out their personal and business bank accounts and taking off to parts unknown with his assistant.

If it wasn't for the money, she wouldn't have cared if she ever saw his smug face again. Her life was much better without him and his controlling, demeaning ways. It was embarrassing, actually, that she'd let herself be treated that way by him. She wouldn't make that mistake again.

Even though his betrayal had put an end to the upscale lifestyle they'd led as real estate developers, she didn't miss it one bit. She loved her new, simpler life running the Beachcomber Motel on the coast of Maine and the promise of a new career, baking pies like the cranberry-apple one she was now retrieving from the windowsill in the kitchen, where she'd left it to cool.

The pie had come out nearly perfect. The fluted crust was golden brown, and the little maple leaves she'd cut out of dough for the top were perfectly formed. It was hard to believe that just a month ago, she couldn't even mix a dough that would stick together. She leaned over and took a deep breath, inhaling the sugary scent of apples and cinnamon.

Cooling a pie in the window, where the fresh sea air could wash over it, was the best way, according to the notes she'd found in her grandmother's recipes, and the kitchen window at the motel had a very wide sill that fit a pie plate perfectly. Maybe her grandmother had even used this window herself, to cool her own pies.

Movement out in the parking lot of the motel caught her eye, and she glanced out, smiling at the colorfully painted motel-room doors and all the cars parked in front of them. She'd been afraid the tourist traffic would dry up after the last big town event, but it hadn't, and the motel was almost full.

A rental car had pulled up in front of Room Eight, and a woman with shoulder-length blond curls was struggling to get a large suitcase out of the trunk. The woman looked to be in her late twenties or early thirties —about Gina's age—and her face seemed familiar. She must have been Deena Walters' daughter, Samantha. They'd given Deena a discount coupon so that her daughter could come and visit.

As she watched, the door to Room Nine opened, and a tall man with short-cropped hair stepped out. He was kind of cute, not that Gina was looking, with a square jaw and friendly smile. Her cousin, Jules, must have checked him in, as Gina had no idea who he was. As she watched, he helped the woman heft her suitcase out of the trunk, and then they stood there chatting. Were they flirting? Maybe there would be a little romance at the Beachcomber Motel this summer.

"That must be Samantha Walters. She checked in online." Jules had come to stand beside her. Her gaze drifted from the flirting couple to the pie. "Wow, that pie looks amazing."

"Thanks!" Gina's heart swelled with pride at her cousin's compliment. It was hard to believe that she'd gone years without speaking to her cousins before they'd inherited the motel and been forced to work together. Now, they were closer than sisters which was another reason that Gina loved her new life in Shell Cove. She had family here. She belonged. "So, the new system is working good, then?"

The old motel used to have regular metal keys on large orange plastic cards to open the rooms. Jules had recently implemented digital locks on a few of the rooms so that people could check in online and get access to their rooms without having to stop by the motel lobby for the key.

Jules nodded. "So far, so good. These are the first two guests."

"Who's the guy?" Gina asked.

"That's Chuck Sullivan's son, Cole."

Gina's eyes widened, and she stared at her cousin. "You put them next to each other?"

Deena Walters and Chuck Sullivan were in their late sixties, a widow and widower who had found love later in life. Unfortunately, their adult children didn't approve. Deena and Chuck had invited their kids for a visit, hoping to show them that they truly were made for each other and win over their approval, but Gina had no idea they were coming at the same time.

"Why wouldn't I put them next to each other? Those are the two rooms that I'm testing the new system on."

"Yeah, but they each don't approve of the other's parent. That sort of puts them in enemy camps. Things could get dicey."

Jules looked back out at the couple, who were now laughing together as if one of them had just come up with the most hilarious joke.

Looks like they're getting along fine to me." She turned and picked the clipboard up off the counter. "I have some last-minute paperwork for Sam to fill out. I'm going to run out and catch her before she settles in. Don't forget we're meeting Maddie at noon to celebrate Gram's birthday lunch at The Boathouse."

Jules headed out into the parking lot, her chocolate curls bouncing as she made her way toward Sam. She'd recently cut her long hair so that it just brushed her shoulders, and it suited her. Gina fiddled with the ponytail that sprouted from the top of her head. She hadn't done anything to her own mousy-brown hair since coming to Shell Cove, and it was a rat's nest. But then, her hair never came out nice like Jules's or her other cousin, Maddie's, who had gorgeous silky blond locks. Better to just stuff it in a ponytail. Gina wasn't too concerned over how she looked.

Mention of their grandmother brought on a pang of sadness. If it wasn't for Gram, she never would have found this idyllic new life. Gram had left the motel to her, Jules, and Maddie. At first, Gina hadn't planned on staying. The last thing she'd wanted was to run a motel in a small seaside town, especially since it involved working with her cousins. Her plan had been to get out as quickly as possible, but the place had grown on her.

On her deathbed, Gram had made her promise to enjoy the simple things in life. Gina hadn't realized what that meant at the time, but after rediscovering her passion for baking and then finding her grandmother's pie recipes, she came to understand why Gram had made her promise. The simple things really were better, and now, more than anything, she wanted to stay in Shell Cove and pursue her passion.

But she wouldn't be able to do that if she didn't find Hugh. She put the pie on the counter, pulled out her phone, and texted the local private investigator who was trying to help her find him. Her office was on the way to The Boathouse restaurant, and Gina was hoping she could stop in and get an update on the case before meeting her cousins for lunch.

Sam slid her sunglasses down on her nose and peered out over the top to check out the backside of the guy in Room Nine as he walked off toward his car. It had been a while since she'd flirted with anyone, and he was kind of cute. But flirting was as far as it would go.

As a divorce attorney, she knew painfully well that most relationships didn't work out. After ten years of witnessing how people who had once vowed to stick together until "death did them part" could screw each other over, she had to admit she'd become a bit jaded.

Maybe she should have gone into the family chocolate business like her mother had wanted. It would be a lot less stress. And now that she was back in Shell Cove, she was reminded of how gorgeous the ocean town was. Moving back and working at Saltwater Sweets had once been something she would never have considered, but now she had to admit the idea held a certain appeal.

But she wasn't here for romance or job opportunities. She was here to save her mother, Deena, from the guy who was trying to steal their family business.

Deena had been gushing about Chuck Sullivan for months now. Sam didn't know who this guy was or when he'd come into the picture, but she was certain that he was up to no good.

Why else would he suddenly swoop in and pretend to be interested in the family business? Sam knew the type. They preyed on widows with a cushy nest egg. Her mom didn't have much money. In fact, she'd had to sell the modest house Sam had grown up in to pay for some of Dad's medical bills. Now, her mother lived in a one-bedroom apartment, hence the reason for Sam to rent a motel room instead of staying with her mother. She loved her mom, but that small apartment was too close quarters. Sam liked her privacy.

Chuck probably didn't realize that her mother had no money, though. Or maybe he was trying to take the business away somehow. Saltwater Sweets was practically famous on the East Coast for its candies, and Sam was sure it was worth quite a bit of money. Her mother was very naïve, and because she was such a sweet person, Sam knew she'd fall for this guy's scam in a heartbeat. Sam needed to protect her.

The hotel door opened, and a woman with a clipboard came toward her.

"Hi! I'm Jules Whittier. Are you Sam?"

Sam pushed the sunglasses back up her nose and smiled at the chipper woman coming toward her. That was another thing about the small towns, the people were always so friendly. Not like at the law firm.

"Yes, I'm Sam."

"Welcome! I just have a little bit of paperwork to fill out on the rental car." Jules pointed at the Toyota that Sam had rented at the airport for the drive out. "It will only take a few minutes."

That was good because Sam only had a few minutes. She was due to meet her mother and this Chuck guy for lunch at some restaurant on the water.

Even though her mother insisted that Chuck was a

nice guy with the best intentions, Sam knew that was how they always acted at first. He probably figured he could buy her a fancy meal to win her over. Well, if he thought she was going to sit there and fawn all over him for a lobster dinner, he had another think coming. She knew just the right questions to ask, to dig down to the root of what he was really up to. Chuck Sullivan wasn't going to know what hit him.

Hopefully, she could nip this romance in the bud and bring her mother back to her senses in a few days and then head back to her stressful life in the city. Surely, it wouldn't take much to expose this scammer's true intentions to her mother.

CHAPTER 2

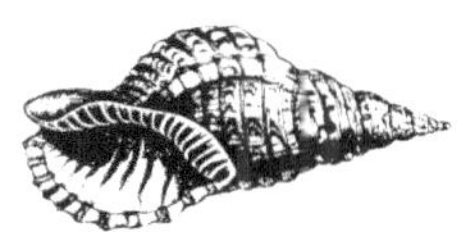

Gina glanced around to make sure no one was watching as she pulled her car into the alleyway that led behind the brick building that housed the offices of Ellison Chandler. The building was on the outskirts of town, and the back parking lot ensured privacy for Ellie's clients.

At first, Gina had been worried about hiring Ellie. From her references, she was a good private investigator, but she was also the daughter of Leena McCain, one of the senior citizens in town that Gina and her cousins had befriended. She didn't want anyone to know that she was searching for Hugh. Her cousins had no idea how her marriage had ended, and she wanted to keep it that way.

Ellie had assured her she was discreet and of course would never divulge a client's name to her mother. So far, no one had mentioned anything about Gina hiring a PI, so she assumed Ellie was true to her word. She'd have to be, or no one would hire her, especially not in this small town, where rumors flourished like fertilized dandelions.

Gina took the back stairway to the second floor. There was only one office there, and Gina stopped for a second in front of the thick oak door with the frosted glass window that had Ellie's name stenciled in gold and black before knocking.

"Come in!"

Ellie's office was as simple and efficient as she was. It was furnished with the basics: an old oak desk with a squeaky Naugahyde chair, rows of metal filing cabinets along one wall, and an old leather Chesterfield sofa along the opposite wall under a row of windows. It looked like Ellie had spent more than one night on that sofa. The only personal item was a framed photograph of a man in a police uniform atop one of the cabinets. The scent of stale coffee lingered in the air.

Ellie was seated behind the desk, her silver-streaked dark hair pulled back. She wore her uniform of a black T-shirt and jeans. Gina had met with her a few times, and she'd always been dressed similarly. A laptop was open to her left, and she had a pile of papers in front of her.

"Hi, Gina. Have a seat." Ellie gestured to a worn chair on the opposite side of the desk, and Gina sat.

"Thanks. How are you?" Gina asked.

"Good. You?" Ellie looked up at Gina with her

sharp blue eyes. Ellie was what Gina's grandmother would have called a "keen observer." She always seemed to be studying her surroundings and the people in them. Gina imagined that was a holdover from the days when Ellie had been a cop and had to rely on observation and instinct to get her job done. Her gaze was a bit intense, and Gina imagined that those blue eyes had elicited a confession from more than one criminal.

"Great." Gina liked Ellie.

She guessed her age at around late forties, too young to be retired from the police force, but Gina had never asked about it. They'd clicked right away but hadn't discussed much about their personal lives, though Ellie knew all about Hugh and his betrayal, of course. They'd only met a few times and hadn't had time to develop a friendship, though Gina felt they could be friends in due time. Ellie was smart and trustworthy, and Gina guessed she had a fun side to her. A sad side, too, Gina had noticed and wondered if that had anything to do with the framed picture on the filing cabinet.

Ellie shuffled the papers and got down to business. "I've made some progress in the case."

Gina's heart flipped. "Did you find Hugh?"

"Not exactly. I traced him and his assistant…" Ellie looked down at the paperwork for reference. "Holly?"

"Yes." Gina frowned as images of the vivacious brunette bubbled up. Gina had thought she and Holly were friends, but apparently the whole time she'd been fooling around with Hugh.

"I traced them to the Cayman Islands. They've been there for a while. Holly has a bank account with eighty grand in it."

"Eighty grand? He took a lot more than that."

Ellie nodded. "I know. They may have spent some of it or invested it or have it in an account I haven't uncovered yet. There are many possibilities, but I'll keep looking."

"So we're a little bit closer to finding him, then?" Gina asked. Anxiety was gnawing at her, and she wasn't exactly sure what she was going to do when they did locate him or how she was going to get her money. She knew he wouldn't just hand it over. Luckily, she had some leverage that she could use to force him if she had to.

"Yes, we are closer, and also, I've learned something from a source I have in law enforcement. The FBI is looking for Hugh."

Gina's heart lurched. The FBI? If they found him, would they take all the money? She supposed the money he'd embezzled from their clients would be confiscated, but surely not what he'd taken out of their personal account.

"The FBI? Sounds serious." Gina wasn't sure how she felt about that. Hugh had stolen money from her and their clients, and he should be punished. At one time, she would have been devastated at the thought of him going to jail, but now all she could muster was a tiny bit of sympathy. That was a good sign. The old Gina would always take Hugh back after he screwed up. Hopefully now, she would be immune to those puppy-dog eyes he turned on her when begging for forgiveness. She needed to stay strong if she wanted her money back.

"Embezzling is a crime. I assume one of your clients has contacted the FBI since Hugh is a fugitive."

"Of course." After Hugh had left, Gina was questioned by local police over and over, but she hadn't realized the case had been escalated to the FBI. "I hope to get to him first. He's not going to be able to transfer money from a jail cell."

"I'm preparing a written report for you, but it won't be ready until later today." Ellie put the paperwork down, her smile faltering as she looked up at Gina. "There's another thing."

"What?"

"Someone is putting out feelers, looking for you."

"Me? Why? Do you think our old clients think I'm involved in whatever Hugh was up to?" After Hugh's disappearance, she'd met with the clients. They'd all seemed convinced she was innocent.

"It could be. They're looking for you under your married name, though. I don't want to scare you, but you might want to be careful."

Another reason it had been a smart move to go back to her maiden name after Hugh disappeared. Even though she'd told her cousins they were divorced, they weren't because she'd never been able to find Hugh to serve him papers.

Gina couldn't help but look over her shoulder as she left Ellie's office. Was someone watching her right now? Who was looking for her? And, more importantly, what would they do if they found her?

CHAPTER 3

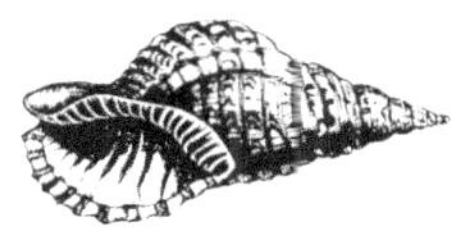

Cole parked his rental car across from The Boathouse restaurant. The old building was clad in worn cedar shakes, but the white trim was crisp and fresh, and the window boxes overflowed with red and white flowers. It had a pleasant view of a small cove complete with lobster boats and dinghies and then the ocean beyond. It looked upscale but not too fancy.

He took a sip of the café Americano he'd purchased at Ocean Brew, the coffee shop in Shell Cove, on his way out of town. He needed something strong to fortify himself for this lunch. Cole loved his coffee, but the stuff that came out of the ancient Mr. Coffee machine at the Beachcomber motel tasted like old canal water.

He supposed the Beachcomber was a decent hotel. The room was kind of kitschy with a shell theme, but it was spotless. The location was certainly nice, right on a little cliff overlooking the ocean. Had he read something about steps to the beach? He'd have to check that out later.

He'd been surprised to strike up a conversation with the girl in the next room. At first, he'd been just trying to be gentlemanly. He'd seen her struggling with the luggage and didn't think twice about offering help. She seemed nice, her smile was friendly, and she had a carefree laugh. When she'd looked at him with those innocent cornflower-blue eyes, he couldn't help but linger.

He wasn't in town for a romance, though, so he wouldn't take it any further. He had bigger fish to fry, like the woman his father had taken up with. Cole had become very close with his father over the past five years since his mother died, and maybe he was being a little overprotective. But the way his father gushed about this Deena Walters person pinged his radar, and his instincts told him something wasn't right. His father was a wealthy man, and Cole knew that he was lonely, but he was also generous and easily taken advantage of. Cole had no intention of letting some gold digger take his dad for everything he was worth.

Besides, he needed a distraction after the catastrophe that had happened at work. Being on a forced vacation was torture, but Cole hadn't handled his last assignment well. Now, the higher-ups were probably mulling over what to do with him. Heck, after what had happened, Cole was mulling over what to do with himself. He'd put his all into that job, was practically married to it, something his ex-wife and subsequent girlfriends always complained about.

Cole finished his coffee and ventured in. He paused just inside the door and scanned the restaurant. The scanning was mostly out of habit, checking out the situation for threats. Of course he didn't need to do that here, but old habits died hard.

He spotted his father at a round table in the corner and headed over, taking his time so that he could assess the woman seated next to him. He supposed she *looked* nice. She was attractive for her age—short blond hair, slim, youthful looking but had probably had some work done—the typical gold-digger type.

Wait, was there a third person at the table? The person was seated with their back to him, but that blond hair… was that the girl from the motel? What was *she* doing here?

His dad glanced over, and his face split into a smile that warmed Cole's heart. His dad jumped up, and Cole rushed over to hug him.

"Son, it's so good to see you!"

"You, too, Dad." Cole held his father's gaze, genuine warmth passing between them, and for just a second, it was just the two of them as it had been these past five years. Then Chuck turned his attention to the table.

"Deena, Sam, I'd like you to meet my son, Cole." Chuck practically glowed with pride. "Sam is Deena's daughter. She's also visiting in town."

Cole turned to face the enemy. He'd been expecting just one, but now there were two. That was okay. He could handle them.

"We've met. Nice to see you again." Cole forced a smile during the introductions, but inwardly, he was making note of their every move.

Of course, now he realized everything that he'd thought was so enchanting about Sam at the motel was wrong. Her carefree laugh now sounded a little *too* carefree. Forced? A nervous cover-up, most likely. Her innocent cornflower-blue eyes were now steely-gray pools of deception.

"What are you having?" Chuck turned to Cole, who hadn't even glanced at the menu yet as he'd been too busy sizing up the enemy.

"The lobster rolls are great here if you like lobster," Deena offered.

"I'm getting the steak." Chuck patted his stomach, and Cole noticed it was still trim. That was good. At least Deena wasn't trying to kill him off with fattening foods.

"That's a great choice," Deena said.

"The lobster roll is a good choice too," Chuck fawned at Deena, and Cole tried not to scrunch his face up in disgust. Was his dad overdoing it a bit? Sure seemed that way.

"I agree," Deena fawned back at Chuck.

Yech.

"We usually agree. That's why we get along so well, isn't it, dear?"

"Yes." Chuck beamed.

Cole glanced at Sam. Her eyes were narrowed at the happy couple. Was she trying to telegraph a message to her mother not to overdo things? Cole hoped so. It was a little sickening.

"I think I'll have a burger," Cole said.

Lunch came, and Cole managed to keep up his end of the small talk. There was more gushing from his father and Deena. It definitely seemed forced. The burger was good, but Cole hardly tasted it. He was too busy trying to keep his gaze from wandering over to Sam as she cut into her steak like a lumberjack that hadn't eaten in months.

It was amusing because Cole was used to dates that barely nibbled at salads. Somehow, Sam managed to chow down the meal in the most feminine way. Her pouty lips puckered as she chewed, and the sunlight coming in from the window highlighted the smattering of freckles across her nose. But Sam wasn't his date. She was the enemy. He bet his dad would pay for lunch, and Sam had ordered one of the most expensive items, second only to the lobster roll her mother had ordered. They were certainly taking advantage of his father's generous nature.

After the meal was done and the dishes cleared, Deena said, "Anyone want to split dessert?" She glanced up from the small dessert menu at Cole.

He was taken aback. He always used to split dessert with his mother. Did Deena know that? He glanced at his father. Had Chuck told her?

"I'm too full." Cole tried to keep his voice light.

"Me too," Chuck said.

"And me." Sam took out her wallet. "Plus, I'm paying, and it will keep the tab down."

"Oh no." Chuck held his hand up. "I've got this."

"Nope. I insist." Sam had already flagged down the waitress and given her card.

Cole had to admit it was a clever maneuver. Offer to pay and make it seem like they weren't after Chuck for his money. They'd probably worked it out ahead of time. It might be harder than he'd first thought to expose their real motivations.

"Well, thank you, Sam." Deena beamed at her daughter. "I was hoping that you two would like to come back to Saltwater Sweets and see some of the enhancements we've made. I want to show you what an asset your father is to the business."

Cole couldn't wait to see that. He just hoped his father hadn't spent a lot of money outfitting the shop already.

CHAPTER 4

Gina relaxed into her chair at The Boathouse restaurant as she perused the menu. The upholstered chairs were comfortable, the water glasses sparkled, and the silverware gleamed. Outside, a seagull swooped in the air as boats bobbed in the cove. She wasn't used to eating in such pleasant surroundings anymore. In her previous life, she'd eaten at fancy restaurants all the time, but now, she could only afford fast food and pizza. She didn't mind. Her life was much better now.

She was happy to splurge for this special occasion, and even though it was marked with the sadness of missing her grandmother, that sadness was overshadowed by the joy of reuniting with her cousins. If it hadn't been for Gram, the three of them would never have come to Shell Cove.

"Isn't that Chuck and Deena over there?" Maddie pointed at a table in the corner.

Chuck, Deena, and their kids were just standing to leave.

"Yep, and Deena's daughter, Sam, and Chuck's son, Cole. The two of them are staying at the Beachcomber."

Maddie's blue eyes widened. "That should be interesting." She glanced back over at the table as they all filed out toward the door. "It looks like they're all getting along well. I know Chuck and Deena were worried about making a good impression for each other's kid."

"Hopefully, things will work out. Deena and Chuck are so nice, and they are adults who shouldn't have to have the kids' approval." Jules shook her head and turned her attention back to the menu. "Sam and Cole are grown adults. I'm sure that once they meet Chuck and Deena, they'll approve."

"And they were flirting in the parking lot of the motel, so maybe they'll have other things on their mind then breaking up their parents' happy relationship." Jules waggled her eyebrows up and down, and they all laughed.

Gina pretended to look at the menu as the conversation turned to small talk about things going on in town and at the Beachcomber, but she was hardly listening or reading the menu. She was busy thinking about what Ellie had just told her. Who would be looking for her, and why? Maybe Hugh had been up to something much worse than she knew about and now it was going to come down on her.

"Earth to Gina."

Gina glanced up sharply from her menu to see her cousins staring at her. Clearly they were expecting an answer to something, but she had no idea what. "Sorry! I was just thinking about… ummm… pie crust!"

The confused looks on her cousins' faces brought on a pang of guilt. She had never told them anything about Hugh. As far as she knew, they still thought she'd had an amicable divorce. They didn't even know he was missing. When she'd first come to Shell Cove, she was barely speaking to Jules and Maddie and intended to leave as soon as she could. But things changed, and now she was afraid that she'd let it go too long and it was too late to tell them.

"I was saying that I'm getting the scallops. Remember how Gram loved those here?" Jules said.

"I'm getting the lobster. What are you getting, Gina?" Maddie asked.

The items on the menu had barely registered in Gina's mind, so she blurted out the first thing to come to mind. "Clam roll, extra tartar sauce."

Maddie and Jules gave her a funny look but didn't say anything. Was that a weird thing to order? Of course it was. This was fancy dining, and even though clam rolls were on the menu, that was better suited to be ordered at the beach clam shack. She should have ordered baked stuffed haddock. Too late now, though, she realized as she repeated the order for the waitress.

Maddie dug a roll out of the basket and slathered it with butter. "So, the digital locks are working out well?"

"So far. I've only done two rooms, but I think we

should expand that to more rooms as funds allow," Jules said.

"Sounds good." Maddie glanced at Gina to get her take, and Gina nodded.

"That will free up some time for all of us." The three of them split up the work involved with running the motel, and checking people in was a big part of that.

"I love running the motel, but more free time that I can spend away from it can't hurt," Maddie said. "I can't believe you are still in the storage room, Gina. Maybe you should think about spending more time away from the motel. I feel like you are doing the bulk of the work, and I want it to be fair for all of us."

Jules nodded. "You should be thinking more about the future and less about the motel. Maybe even thinking about getting your own place. Sure, we still need to run the Beachcomber, but we can do other things too. Like your pies. After all, Maddie and I are thinking about our futures, and you should too."

More guilt surfaced. She hadn't told her cousins that she wanted to open the pie shop in town because that would mean she would have to explain the whole mess with Hugh and the money. The old saying her grand-mother used to say about weaving a tangled web when you try to deceive came to mind.

Gina shrugged. "I don't mind staying in the storage room. I have it fixed up pretty nice, and I am available if any of the guests needs me."

"I don't know." Maddie looked concerned. "I don't

like the way you leave that place unlocked at night while you're in there all alone."

Gina laughed. "Here in Shell Cove? There's never any crime, so there's nothing to worry about. Anyway, speaking of getting our own places, how are things going in Starfish Cottage?"

Maddie had recently bought her dream cottage on the beach. It was small but actually had its own name, Starfish Cottage. It had been uninhabited for over a decade and needed a lot of work, but Maddie had already worked wonders with it.

Maddie's eyes lit up. "We're practically finished. It'll be just a few weeks now. That's why I haven't had either of you over." Maddie's expression turned apologetic. "I want to wait until you can see it fully done."

"I did notice that Dex was spending a lot of time over there. The renovation bill must be sky-high," Jules teased.

Maddie had started dating the local handyman, Dex Wheeler. Despite a rocky start to their relationship, the two seemed to have hit it off.

Maddie blushed. "Very funny. Rumor about town is that you're spending so much time at Nick Barlowe's place that you're hardly ever at the motel. Is that true, Gina?"

Gina laughed at the good-natured ribbing her cousins were giving one another. Nick worked at the bank, and from day one, it had been obvious to everyone, except maybe him and Jules, that they belonged together.

"She's not in her room that much. Maybe we should rent it out," Gina joked.

Jules lived in one of the motel rooms, but Gina didn't think she was ready to move in with Nick right away.

Jules grabbed a roll and deflected their teasing by turning the conversation to one of their favorite motel guests. "I always make sure I get my motel work done. Speaking of which, Aggie Fletcher isn't going to be there much longer. She's looking for a place in town. It looks like things with her and Henry are going very smoothly."

Gina smiled at that. Aggie was a colorful character that had checked into the motel when they'd had a cooking contest. She'd met Nick's grandfather, Henry, and the two of them hit it off and made the cutest couple.

"Having Aggie as a long-term resident was great and helped with finances, but now we're getting more and more bookings, so it shouldn't hurt us."

"Yeah, bookings are really up," Jules said. "We're filled the next ten weekends and partially filled for the weekdays." Jules patted Maddie on the arm. "Looks like your last event really turned on the faucet for the tourists."

"I've noticed more tourists in town and all the business owners seem very happy about that," Maddie said. Maddie was the head of the Chamber of Commerce, a part-time job that she took very seriously. She'd been responsible for organizing a few events that had gotten tourists talking about Shell Cove, but she wasn't stopping there. Lately, she had been surveying the business owners and trying to figure out how to keep things running smoothly in Shell Cove and how to keep the tourists coming.

"How is everything going with plans for the town celebration?" Gina asked.

As part of her job, Maddie was in charge of organizing a big picnic to celebrate the town's 250th anniversary.

"Really good. Everything is falling into place. There's going to be a parade and games and maybe fireworks in the town common." Maddie said.

"And naturally, there will be signature dishes." Jules's comment had them all laughing.

When they'd first come to town, their first visitors to the motel had been three senior ladies, Pearl, Rose, and Leena. They'd been friends of their grandmother and had come with a huge welcome basket. The cousins had become good friends with the older women and referred to them as the "welcome wagon ladies." Rose, Pearl, and Leena seemed to always have a hand in all the town goings-on and insisted on people bringing signature homemade dishes to each event. In fact, it was Pearl who had encouraged Gina to open the pie shop. Gina's pies always got compliments. Maddie and Jules weren't as lucky in the signature-dish department.

"I'm sure you'll make a pie, Gina," Jules said. "I'm going to have to think hard on what to do. I don't want to fall out of favor with those ladies."

Gina and Maddie laughed.

Jules turned to Maddie. "Easy for you to laugh. You won't fall out of favor—you're dating Rose's grandson!"

Maddie looked sheepish. "I'm sure Rose doesn't play favorites. I just hope we have the same amount of energy as those ladies when we get to be their age."

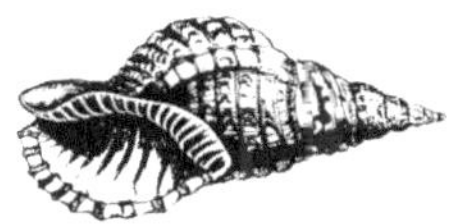

CHAPTER 5

Rose Wisnewski sat on the bench across from the row of quaint shops in Shell Cove, eating her pistachio ice cream and reflecting on how good life was.

How fortunate was she to be in such good health in her early eighties and have two of her best friends right beside her?

She glanced over at Pearl and Leena. Sure, they had a few wrinkles and some gray hair, but for the most part, the three of them were in good health. Not only that, but their beloved town of Shell Cove had been revitalized and was coming back to life again. She couldn't ask for much more than that.

"Look at all the tourists." Pearl waved her spoon at the quaint shops across the street.

The trim had been freshly painted, new colorful awnings shaded the windows, and lush flowers overflowed the window boxes and planters along the street.

Tourists in flip-flops and sunglasses strolled down the street with bags of souvenirs.

"It seems like more tourists are coming every day," Rose said. "I think naming Maddie to head the chamber of conference was a good idea."

"She's doing a good job on the town picnic too." Leena shoved the last of her cone into her mouth and crunched down on it.

She was always the first to finish her ice cream. Pearl, who daintily took tiny bites from her cup, was always the last. Rose was in the middle.

"She's got some fun events," Leena said. "But I think we should have more cornhole setups."

"Oh, I love cornhole!" Pearl said. "Do you think we could get bocce in?"

Leena scrunched up her face. "They'd have to dig up the grass to put in a bocce court, Pearl."

Pearl looked disappointed. "I suppose, but it would be fun. Bocce is one of my favorites."

"Speaking of favorites," Rose cut in, "what are you bringing?"

"I'm bringing triple-chocolate layer cake," Pearl said.

"Deviled eggs, of course," Leena said, as if she would bring anything else. For twenty-five years, she'd been bringing deviled eggs to almost every town event. It was her signature dish.

"I'm bringing potato salad," Rose said. "And I gave my macaroni salad recipe to Dex. He and Maddie have been seeing a lot of each other lately, and they wanted to make something special together."

Rose had been overjoyed when Dex and Maddie had started dating. She hadn't liked Dex's previous girlfriend, Lorelei, very much. She never said anything to Dex as she didn't want to interfere, but Lorelei just wasn't right for him. Not to mention Lorelei had wanted him to move away to Portland, and Rose would have missed him terribly. The two were very close, so having him stay in Shell Cove was a bonus, but mostly, she was happy that Dex was with the right girl.

"Things are really looking up in town since Maddie and her cousins came," Pearl said.

"Brought new life to the place," Rose added.

"Except maybe a little bit more than we bargained for," Leena said. "I still think it's a little suspicious that I saw Gina with my Ellie. But you know Ellie. She won't say a word about why they were together, and trust me, I've tried to get it out of her. She just shrugs and says they're friends, but I think Gina has hired her to investigate something."

Pearl took another tiny scoop of ice cream. "It's probably none of our business, Leena."

"I suppose." Leena sighed, her gaze drifting to Saltwater Sweets, the chocolate shop across the street. "Oh look. It's Deena and Chuck. That must be Chuck's son. Is that Samantha? She's gotten even more lovely. I haven't seen her in years. Such a nice young girl. Remember when she helped me out when I broke my leg?"

"Of course we remember. She is a very nice girl," Pearl agreed.

"She's a grown woman now. I wonder if she's still as nice," Rose said. "Sometimes life makes people jaded."

"It appears as if they are all getting along, but Chuck and Deena still look worried. Maybe things aren't going so good," Leena said.

Rose turned to look at her. "You still think you can win that bet?"

In addition to butting in on town events, welcoming newcomers, and making signature dishes, the three women entertained themselves by making bets on whether the various potential couples in town would get together, stay together, or break up.

Pearl also turned to Leena. "That reminds me, don't you owe us for the Mex bet? Maddie and Dex are very chummy these days."

Leena snorted. "Don't be so hasty. Let's wait and see if it's going to stick."

"Trust me. It will stick. Have you seen them together?" Rose asked.

Across the street, Chuck, Deena, Sam, and Cole were entering the shop. Saltwater Sweets was a cute little shop in one of the town's oldest buildings. It was a family business, having been started by Deena's great grandmother. The front had two large windows loaded with displays of thick chunks of fudge and decadent-looking chocolates on triple-tier displays.

Since Chuck had come into Deena's life, Deena was happier than Rose had seen her in years, and the shop had been flourishing. Deena had let it go after her husband died, and it had fallen into disrepair, but now she and Chuck had worked hard to bring it back up to speed.

Chuck was good for Deena. Rose hoped Samantha and Cole would see that. Of course, she and Pearl and Leena were doing everything they could to try to help Deena and Chuck make Sam and Cole realize they were perfect for each other.

Pearl spooned up a tiny blob of ice cream. "Maybe Sam and Cole will get together. Anyone in on a bet? Would we call it Sole or Cam?"

The three ladies named their bets based on a mash-up of the couple's names.

Leena shook her head and nodded toward the shop. "Maybe not. Look at the body language. I don't think Sam and Cole will be turning into a couple, and maybe Deena and Chuck won't be one after this visit is over, either."

CHAPTER 6

"**I** think Chuck's done very well at mastering the little swirls that we put on top of each of the different types of chocolates. You remember how difficult that is, don't you, Sam?"

Sam remembered. She also remembered that it was her father that used to put the swirls on. Seeing Chuck do it made her heart lurch. She wasn't jealous, that would be ridiculous. She was a mature adult and understood that her father had been gone for many years and her mother deserved to find someone to be happy with. But not Chuck, because Chuck was obviously trying to take advantage.

"And he's bringing the business into the twenty-first century. He's revamped the website and is modernizing everything on the computer. He's even installed new software we can use for inventory and accounting," Deena said proudly.

Sam frowned. Chuck had been doing computer

work? "Mom, I would've been happy to help with the computer and install new software for you."

"I didn't want to bother you, dear. I know how busy you are." Deena turned to Chuck and Cole. "Sam is multitalented. She's not only a brilliant lawyer. She's good with computers too."

Sam brushed off the compliment, embarrassed. The truth was she really wasn't that great with computers, but she was a far sight better than either of her parents had been. And as a lawyer, she was far from brilliant, though she had saved several women from getting taken advantage of in many divorce cases.

Guilt bubbled up. Her mother had given up on asking her to come out and help with the business, and that was her own fault. She'd never made Saltwater Sweets a priority. Every time her mother had asked for her help, she'd put it off, always too busy with her cases.

Maybe she had only herself to blame that Chuck had insinuated himself into the business. That was all the more reason for her to get her mother to see the light. It sounded like he had access to the accounting and bank accounts. Hopefully, he hadn't started moving things into his own name. She made a mental note to check out the computer and see what he'd been up to. Her mother was way too trusting.

She glanced over at Cole and caught him looking at her with his sapphire-blue eyes. Those eyes had looked warm and kind in the parking lot, but now they were as cold as a shark's. Was he sizing her up, trying to figure out if he could pull the wool over her eyes as easily as they had done with her mother? Well, if he thought that was gonna be the case, he had another think coming.

It wasn't lost on Sam that when her mother mentioned that she was a lawyer, Chuck and Cole had remained silent about his profession. That would have been the perfect time for Chuck to talk proudly about all his son's accomplishments, but the two had been mute, which made her wonder what exactly Cole did for a living. Perhaps he was a professional con man like his father. She should probably research them both on the internet.

Her mother was still going on about Chuck as if he were some sort of chocolate-making genius. "And I taught Chuck how to temper the chocolate," she turned adoring eyes on Chuck, "another skill he picked up very quickly."

Chuck laughed. "I think you're giving me too much credit. It's the teacher that the credit should go to, and that's you."

Sam almost gagged as they gazed into each other's eyes.

"He's done a great job with the displays too." Her mother gestured toward the candy displays throughout the store. The various racks, shelves, and oak display cases had been in the same configuration since before Sam was born. She'd noticed right away that they'd been moved around, and now, knowing that it was Chuck's doing made her feel resentful. But she did have to admit this arrangement worked better.

"We put the more popular items at eye level and the

things that kids like on the lower shelves." Chuck looked at her almost as if for approval.

"I think it was a great idea. In fact, we've agreed on every single change that was made to the store." Deena's tone sounded a little bit forced.

Sam pulled her gaze from the displays to look at her mother. The way she and Chuck were fawning over each other was a bit over the top.

But Sam had to admit the soft look in their eyes made it seem like they were truly smitten with each other, and not just her mother. Chuck had that look too. Maybe he was a good actor.

Sam felt a little tinge of jealousy. She'd had many boyfriends over the past years, but she didn't think any of them had looked at her quite that way.

Was it her imagination, or did her mom seem nervous? Why would that be? Had she done something stupid like handing the title to the property over to Chuck, and now she was afraid Sam wouldn't approve? She needed to get her mother alone and get some answers to these questions. She certainly couldn't ask them with Chuck and Cole hovering like hawks watching a henhouse.

As Chuck and her mother rambled on about how quickly Chuck had taken to chocolate making, how wonderful Deena was at teaching, and how they agreed on everything, Sam let her gaze wander over the shop. A new picture was up on the wall. It looked like one of the first pictures of it. A woman in early-1900s garb was making chocolate in this very room, but the room was fairly empty. The woman must have been Sam's great-great-grandmother, who had started the business. The fact that the business had been built by her family hit her with a force she hadn't felt before, and her determination not to lose it to Chuck surged.

Next to that was a photograph from ten years ago that made her heart squeeze. Her mother, her father, and she were on their sailboat, all smiles as the sun set behind them. She stepped a little closer to the picture. Her dad had loved sailing, and they'd done that as a family almost every weekend. Was the old boat still in storage? They'd put it away when her father had gotten sick, and they never had a chance to sail on it again.

"Your family likes to sail too?" Sam jumped. Cole had sneaked up and was standing beside her, gazing at the picture himself.

"Too? You mean you guys sail?"

A shadow flickered across Cole's face, and he nodded. "We used to when my mom was alive, but after she died, there were just too many memories."

Sam felt a slight bond forming amidst a tug of sympathy. What a strange coincidence… hey, wait a minute! That would be just the type of thing a scammer would say to try to create a bond.

"We were hoping you guys would come to the town celebration picnic this Saturday with us," Deena was saying from her spot behind the counter. "It'll be so much fun. We'll be like one happy family."

One happy family? Sam didn't think so, but she bit

her tongue. Her mother looked so excited about it. How could she refuse?

"That sounds great, Mom. I'd love to."

"Me too." Cole's voice was tinged with hesitation. Maybe he didn't want to spend that much time with her, knowing that she would see right through him.

"I'll be bringing a variety of chocolates, of course, and I was wondering if you'd like to help me make them tomorrow, Sam." Her mother looked at her hopefully, and Sam's heart melted. As a child, she'd made chocolates with her mother and grandmother often, but she hadn't done any of that in years. Comforting family memories bubbled up, and she was surprised at how much she really did want to make chocolates with her mom.

"Cole, I was hoping you'd want to go golfing with me. We'll leave the ladies to making the chocolates. I don't want to show them up," Chuck joked.

Even better, thought Sam. Chuck and Cole would be out of the way, and she could get her mother alone and get answers to the questions she'd been waiting to ask.

"I'd love to. That sounds great." Sam checked her watch. She had a conference call with a client in an hour. "I have to get back to the motel room and get some work done. But it was great meeting you, Chuck and Cole. We'll talk later, Mom?"

"Of course." Though she had expected her mother to look disappointed, her expression looked closer to relief.

"I've got to run too," Cole said. "It was great meeting you all, and I'm sure I will be seeing you soon. Thanks for lunch, Sam. Next one's on me."

They left at the same time, with Cole holding the door open for her. It was a sweet, gentlemanly gesture, but with him, there was probably an ulterior motive. They got in their separate cars and eyed each other warily like boxers at the end of a round before driving off.

Dread swirled in Deena's stomach as she peered out the front window of Saltwater Sweets and watched her daughter and Cole drive off.

"I don't think our kids are on board with us being together." She turned worried eyes to Chuck.

Chuck snugged a comforting arm around her shoulders and pulled her close. "Now, now, it's only day one. They'll come around. Give it time."

Chuck's steady voice and kindly smile didn't do much to soothe her nerves. "Maybe. Though I don't think they like each other very much, either."

"They just met. They'll get along fine after a few days." Chuck glanced uneasily out the window as if doubting his own optimism. "Maybe we should team them up for some of the games at the town celebration. That will create a sense of camaraderie between them. You know, being on the same side and everything."

"That's a good idea. Cole seems like a very nice young man. I don't know why they wouldn't get along."

Chuck smiled, and she could tell he was pleased at her compliment of his son. "I think it's hard for both of them to see their parent with someone else. Neither one of us has dated, and now, it brings up a lot of feelings for them. Even though they are adults, they still have those childhood feelings about their parents. That never goes away. Sam is a very nice girl with a good head on her shoulders. I'm sure she wants to see you happy and will give us her blessing."

"Yeah, you're probably right." Deena was starting to feel a little better about it now.

"And don't forget we have that surprise. That's bound to bring us all closer together."

Deena smiled up at Chuck. He'd worked hard to make things perfect for this visit with their children. And what he said made sense, but she still had some lingering doubts. Even though Cole seemed nice, she could feel the disapproval radiating from him.

"My offer to share dessert backfired with Cole," Deena said.

Chuck pressed his lips together. It had been his idea. "Maybe it was too soon for that. Don't worry. Some time alone with each of our kids tomorrow is sure to loosen things up."

Deena felt nervous at the idea of time alone with Sam. Normally, she would relish that, but she knew her daughter pretty well, and she'd sensed some serious misgivings about her relationship with Chuck.

She'd foolishly thought that Sam would take to Chuck right away, but she hadn't. And Sam was a smart girl with a good head on her shoulders. She was a divorce attorney who knew about relationships. Had Sam seen something about this relationship that Deena had been blind to?

No. Chuck was probably right, and it was just a shock to Sam to see her with another man besides her father. Things would all turn out fine in a couple of days. Deena was sure of it.

CHAPTER 7

The strawberry-rhubarb pie was cooling in the window, and Gina was just about to retrieve it when she saw Sam and Cole pull in. They parked at opposite ends of the parking lot, got out of their cars, and entered their rooms without even a nod to each other. That did not bode well for Deena and Chuck, but Gina had bigger problems to think about, like why someone would be searching for her.

She slid the pie from the windowsill and frowned at what she saw. The edge of the piecrust that had been facing out was crumbled off. What the heck? She looked out the window to see if it had crumbled onto the ground, but nothing was there. Maybe an animal had scurried off with it already. Had she made the crust too dry? Perhaps all this stress of trying to find Hugh was affecting her pie-making abilities. She made a mental note to pay more attention when making the next one.

Ellie Chandler would be here soon, and she didn't

want to serve pie that looked like it had been nibbled on. She cut it into slices and arranged it on a nice pie dish, leaving the pieces that had the crumbled edges in the fridge. Then she mixed up some fresh lemonade and carried it all out onto the back porch, where they could sit in the comfortable wicker furniture and gaze out at the ocean.

She settled into the wicker rocker and thought about what Ellie had told her as she arranged the plates, glasses, and pitcher on a low table in front of a settee. Why would someone be looking for *her*? Was it someone whom Hugh had screwed over, thinking that she might be part of it? A powerful real estate investor had a lot of money in a project, and Hugh had taken it all. Gina had heard rumors he was tied to organized crime, and if that was true, they might not wait for the law to get even.

Hopefully, that person would know that it was Hugh who had taken everything.

Well… not *everything*. She had kept one document in a safety deposit box. She wasn't even sure why, but when she'd found it in the safe in Hugh's home office, she knew it was something important even if she had no idea what it meant. She'd instinctively known that maybe it was a bad idea to give the documents to the police who had come around with so many questions. And now, she felt that at least she had a little bit of leverage to force Hugh to do the right thing.

Thinking of Hugh dragged her down, so she pushed those thoughts aside and focused on her new future. Her life now was so much better. It was less complicated, happier. The old Gina would have been too scared to stand on her own and think about a future just for her. Had she changed that much? She hoped so.

Ellie pulled into the motel lot, and Gina waved her over to the porch. She took the large manila envelope Ellie handed her and stuffed it behind the cushion. Neither one of her cousins was at the motel today, but in case one of them came in, she didn't want to have to answer any questions about it.

At Ellie's questioning look, she said, "I'd like to keep this on the down low."

Ellie nodded. "I understand. I'll keep to small talk if anyone comes over. I have some feelers out, trying to find the person looking for you. I'll keep you updated."

"Thanks. Please have some pie and lemonade." Gina slid a slice of pie onto one of the smaller plates and poured some lemonade into a tumbler.

Ellie hesitated. "You didn't have to go to any trouble."

"It's no trouble." Gina handed the pie over, and Ellie settled back in her chair.

"Well, if you insist. I've heard such great things about your pies from my mom." Ellie eagerly forked up a piece of pie, her eyes closing as she chewed. That fluttery feeling that Gina got when someone was so obviously enjoying eating one of her pies settled in Gina's stomach.

"Delicious. I hope you are making pie for the town picnic."

Gina laughed. "Of course. Half the town would be disappointed if I didn't."

Ellie took another bite of pie and glanced around as she chewed. "The motel looks really great now. You guys have done a fantastic job."

Gina's heart swelled with pride. "Thank you. We have a tight budget, but we're doing what we can."

"It's a big improvement. In fact, the whole town has really come alive, and I hear that's thanks to you and your cousins."

"Well, to be fair, your mother, Rose, and Pearl had a lot to do with it," Gina said.

"Those three busybodies do come in handy some-times," Ellie said affectionately.

"They have done a lot to help revive the town. They really care about it."

"They do. They're good eggs. Your grandmother was too. I remember her from when she lived in town and used to get up to shenanigans with my mother. She'd be proud of what you guys have done here."

Gina felt a twinge of nostalgia for her grandmother. It was bittersweet, knowing her grandmother would be proud but wasn't here to see their success.

Gina was about to ask more about her grandmother's younger days in Shell Cove when a voice carried over from the side of the motel.

"Ellie Chandler? Is that you?"

Sam shaded her eyes from the setting sun and squinted toward the porch on the ocean side of the Beachcomber Motel. She hadn't seen Ellie Chandler in quite a few years, but Ellie still looked pretty much the same.

"Samantha Walters?" Ellie's questioning look told Sam that *she* didn't look the same.

It was no surprise. Sam had been in her early twenties when she'd last seen Ellie, and she'd changed quite a bit, growing out of her crazy twenties into a mature thirtysomething.

"Yes! How have you been?" Sam rushed up onto the porch, and the two women hugged each other.

Sam had fond memories of Ellie. As one of the town cops when Sam was a teenager, Ellie had been strict but kind, willing to look the other way on a few occasions because she knew Sam and her friends were good kids. When Leena had broken her leg and Ellie had been busy with policing, Sam had helped out with housework and errands and even driving Leena to the doctor's a few times. The two women had grown close despite the age gap.

"You look great. What are you doing here?" Ellie asked.

"I came to visit my mom. I'm staying at the motel." Sam gestured toward the Beachcomber. "You're looking good too."

Ellie waved off the compliment.

"Why don't you join us for some pie?" Gina pointed at the low table, where a plate full of pie slices sat beside a pitcher of lemonade.

"Oh, I don't want to interrupt anything. I just saw Ellie and wanted to say hi," Sam said.

"You're not interrupting anything. We were just chatting." Gina quickly transferred a piece of pie onto one of the smaller plates and gestured for her to sit in one of the wicker chairs.

It was a stroke of luck. Sam really had just wanted to say hi to Ellie, but now that she'd been invited to chat, there was no harm in trying to subtly tap her brain for some of the latest PI techniques on digging into someone's background.

"So how is the private investigator business going?" Sam wasn't sure why Ellie had quit being a cop, but she heard she was very successful as a PI.

"It's going good," Ellie said. "How is lawyering?"

Sam shrugged. "It's okay. It can be a little trying since I work mostly on divorces. You know, the darker side of human nature and all that."

Ellie and Gina both nodded as if they knew exactly what she was talking about.

"I see a lot of that in my job too," Ellie said.

"I'll bet. I guess our jobs are somewhat similar in that we have to dig into people's sordid pasts." Sam slid her fork into the pie and took a bite. The crust was soft and flaky, and the filling was just the right mixture of sweet from the strawberries and sugar and sour from the rhubarb. "Yummm. It's delicious."

"Thank you." Gina seemed pleased, if a bit shy at the compliment.

"Anyway, we probably use a lot of the same tools."

Sam tried to sound casual, as if she was just being conversational.

"Probably. Do you use the government finder database?" Ellie asked.

"Sometimes." Sam actually had no idea what that was. "And that other one… the one that has easier access." Sam made a face as if trying to recall the name. She had no idea if there even was an easier one, but she hoped so. The government finder sounded too official.

"Goodchecks or Safechecks?" Ellie said. "They're both easier if you have the Social Security number, which I imagine you would have for your client's spouses."

"Yes, that's it. Safechecks." Sam focused on her pie, unable to look Ellie in the eye because she felt so guilty about lying. "We don't use them too often, but sometimes, you have to."

"I'm surprised you can find out so much just by googling people." Ellie shook her head. "You wouldn't believe the personal information people put on the internet. Especially social media."

"Yeah, tell me about it," Sam laughed.

She noticed Gina's gaze had drifted toward something behind her, and she turned. Her heart leapt. Cole was skulking along the walkway.

How long had he been there, and had he been lurking there at the corner of the house, spying on them?

CHAPTER 8

ole studied the women on the porch. He knew Samantha, of course, and Gina the motel owner, but who was the third woman? It didn't escape his notice that Sam stopped talking abruptly as soon as she saw him. Had she been talking about something they didn't want him to overhear?

The conversation hadn't sounded too serious though, he thought, as he recalled Sam's melodic laughter drifting around the side of the motel before he'd come around the corner. No. Not melodic, he reminded himself. It was more like an evil cackle.

She wasn't laughing now. In fact, she wasn't even smiling. She was scowling at him with her dark, suspicious eyes.

It made him uncomfortable, and he tried not to fidget.

Actually, if he'd known the three women were on

the porch, he would've found a different path to the beach, but he hadn't seen them until it was too late.

And now they were all staring at him, so he had to do something. He plastered a charming smile on his face and approached the edge of the porch.

"Hello there, I was just making my way down to the beach." Cole tilted his head in the direction of the ocean.

"It's a beautiful day for beach walking," Gina said. "Would you like some pie and lemonade before you head out?"

Cole's gaze darted to the table, which held a plate full of pie slices and a pitcher of lemonade. Had the three women simply been having an innocent snack?

The last thing he wanted to do was join them.

"Thanks for the offer, but I'll just go ahead with my walk. You ladies have a nice afternoon." Cole couldn't get out of there quickly enough. He walked over toward the steps to the beach, now feeling uncomfortable as he could feel their gazes burning into his back.

As soon as his feet hit the sand, Cole felt a sense of relaxation. He couldn't see the beach from the motel, and the long swath of white sand that stretched as far as the eye could see was even prettier than he'd imagined.

Once he was out of earshot of the motel, he pulled out his phone and dialed his coworker. Well, technically, Gary wasn't a coworker right now since Cole wasn't actually on active duty. He was on an "extended vacation," or at least, that's how his bosses back at the FBI put it.

It wasn't as if he'd screwed up. There was no way he could've saved that second kidnapped child. But the fact that he hadn't been able to save her weighed heavily on him and messed with his mind. Cole had become overly cautious, and he'd lost his enthusiasm for the job. That would come back in time, at least, that's what the psychologist said.

"Hey, buddy, how's it going?" Gary's voice was jovial, but Cole heard an undercurrent of concern.

"Right now, I'm on a gorgeous beach, looking at the ocean, so I'd say it's going pretty good." Cole didn't want anyone to know how lost he was. He felt like he was at a crossroads, trying to decide whether he should quit for good or dive back in full force. He knew one thing, there was no way he could go back to his under-cover job unless he was all in. People's lives depended on his full concentration on the job.

"How are things back at the ranch?" Cole asked.

"Same old, same old. Things never change." Cole heard the shuffle of papers, and then Gary said, "What's the name of that place where you are visiting your dad? Is it Shell Cove?"

Cole's Spidey sense prickled. "Yeah. Why?"

"There's a little something that could be brewing up your way."

"Here?" Cole couldn't imagine what the FBI's interest would be in this sleepy little seaside town. But he had to admit a certain bit of excitement bubbled up. Was he excited to be back in the chase? He supposed that depended on exactly what the "little something" Gary was talking about entailed.

"Yep. Just a little blip that came across the desk. Seems there might be a fugitive to be on the lookout for in that town."

"Interesting…" Cole let his voice trail off, hoping for more information. He wasn't sure what Gary was getting at and didn't dare ask if they wanted him to help out, for fear that Gary would say no.

"Nobody dangerous or too exciting. Not drugs or murder or kidnapping. Something to do with embezzling, but since it's international, the **FBI** is keeping an eye on it. It's not enough to assign anyone to, but if you're interested, the big boss says you could keep a lookout, you know, sort of on the down low because you're on vacation and all."

Cole could tell by the tone in Gary's voice that he was feeling about, trying to find out if he was ready to accept even the smallest of tasks.

"I could do that. Do you have particulars?" Cole blurted out with an eagerness that surprised even himself. Apparently, he was ready to take on a small task. The truth was he'd been going stir crazy without any work to do, and this sounded like a great way to ease his way back to work and figure out if he wanted to continue police work.

"Yeah, I'll send it to you. Cap says just look around. Don't make an arrest or anything," Gary said.

"How could I? I'm on vacation. I didn't bring my badge."

They both laughed just like usual times, and Cole felt a semblance of normalcy coming back. This was exactly what he needed.

Cole disconnected and continued down the beach, feeling more optimistic than he had in weeks.

The sun was setting, and the sky above the ocean was backlit with hues of baby blue and pink. The sound of the surf soothed him.

He spotted a large piece of driftwood and headed over to sit on it. Taking a deep breath of salty air, he let himself relax further. This was almost like meditating, just like the department psychologist had suggested he do. Maybe she was onto something.

But then thoughts of the reason why he was really in Shell Cove crowded in, and his relaxation vanished. Deena had put on a good act, but he knew deep down that she was not what she was pretending to be.

Now that he'd seen Chuck and Deena together, though, he was afraid that convincing his dad of that fact might be more difficult than he'd anticipated.

CHAPTER 9

Gina stood at the sink with a coffee cup pressed to her lips and squeezed her eyes shut. Her lack of sleep was all Maddie's fault! After her cousin had planted the seed in her head about it being dangerous to stay in the motel alone with the doors unlocked, Gina had spent the whole night imagining she'd heard someone outside. She'd even gotten up at 2:00 a.m. and locked the doors.

Her conversation with her cousins had also impressed on her how she needed to get moving with her plans for the future. She'd noticed a few new shops spring up in town and was worried that someone might rent the old bakery, so she'd messaged the owner late last night.

A reply was sitting in her inbox, and she held her breath as she read it. Good news—the shop was still available, and it had an apartment above that the owner would let her rent at a discount if she rented the shop.

Now, more than ever, she needed to find Hugh before this opportunity passed her by.

She drained the coffee and went to unlock the door.

Oh crap! She'd left a pie in the window. Kind of silly to lock the door but leave the window open like that. Clearly, she needed to work on her home security skills.

She pulled the pie in, frowning as she saw the entire crust on one side was missing.

That was odd because, after the last pie crust incident, she'd made sure to pay close attention when she'd made this crust. The missing crust was way more than would have just crumbled off.

Gina craned to look out the window to see if there was any crust in the flower bed below. There was none, but the impatiens looked trampled. An animal? Gina eyed the pie dubiously. If some kind of animal had been nibbling on it, she'd have to throw it out.

The door to Room Eight opened. Sam came out carrying a rolled-up yoga mat. She was dressed in a loose T-shirt and yoga pants. She looked both ways furtively then crouched low and scurried past Room Nine. That was the room Cole was in. Was she hiding from him?

How amusing.

Gina tossed out the pie, unlocked the door, and shut the window. More movement caught her eye. This time, it was the door to Room Nine.

Cole stepped out with one of the large striped beach towels they supplied slung over his shoulder. He glanced over at Sam's room, a scowl on his face, then hurried off in the direction of the beach.

Even more amusing. It looked like the two of them were avoiding each other, but now they would end up on the beach together.

CHAPTER 10

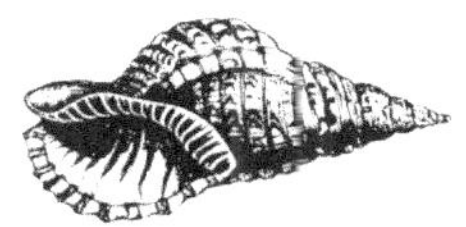

There was nothing more relaxing than yoga on the beach, Sam thought, as she shifted to the downward dog position. Breathing in the fresh sea air, listening to the soothing sound of the lapping waves, and having the whole beach to yourself to focus on the practice all alone was paradise.

Whoops, not quite alone. A movement behind her caught her eye, and she peered upside down through her legs to see who it was.

Darn it! It was Cole. Had he followed her down here?

There went her relaxing morning yoga session. But wait… maybe she could work this to her advantage. This might be a perfect time to ask him some questions. She was no crack interrogator, but she'd learned a few techniques on the job.

Cole hesitated at the bottom of the steps. Probably

because she had her butt in the air and was looking through her legs at him.

"Oh. Good morning," he said as if he hadn't been expecting her to be there.

Sam adjusted her position to something more modest. "Morning. Beautiful day. What brings you down here?"

As if she didn't know he'd followed her.

He glanced down the beach as if deciding how far away from her to get. "Meditating."

"There's a great spot right over there." Sam indicated a spot about six feet from her. "The view from here is gorgeous."

Cole frowned. He eyed the spot uncertainly, then as if making a decision, he strode over and plopped down the towel.

Was he going to meditate on the towel? Seemed like you would get a little bit sandy.

"Maybe you should think about getting a yoga mat if you meditate when you travel. You can roll them up. Takes a bit of room in the luggage, but worth it. It would be more comfortable."

"The towel is fine." Cole sat down on it as if to illustrate how fine it was.

Sam fluidly moved into the cobra position. "So, your dad must really miss your mom." Was that a good question to start with? She knew to start off with innocent friendly questions and then move into the hard stuff.

Cole, who had been trying unsuccessfully to bend

his legs into a pretzel, glanced over. "Of course. Doesn't your mom miss your dad?"

"Of course she does. She hasn't dated anyone else. Has your dad had a lot of girlfriends?"

Cole frowned. "No. Your mom is the first one. It's funny, though, he's really taken to that chocolate shop. I wonder why she hasn't improved it before, though. Hasn't your family owned it all this time?"

Sam's warrior-pose footing faltered. Why was he asking that question? How much should she tell him? The truth probably wouldn't hurt. "After my dad died, she kind of got into a funk."

But now more than ever she was convinced he was up to something. Because if he really did come here just to meditate, then why did he keep asking questions?

Cole nodded. "I guess that's understandable." Cole took a deep breath, placed his hands palm up on his knees, and looked out at the ocean. He actually did know something about meditation, apparently. But Sam wasn't about to give up on her questioning. She was working her way to the questions she really wanted answers to.

"It's nice that your dad is helping out, but he can't really be interested in making chocolate, can he?"

Cole glanced over at Sam. What kind of question was that? He had to admit, though, that he'd been wondering himself if his dad was really that interested in making chocolates. He was making a good effort, but it was probably just to please Deena. But the way Sam asked, it was almost as if she was suspicious of him.

"It seems like he is." Cole noticed that she hadn't really answered his question about why her mother didn't improve the shop before.

His leg was starting to cramp, so he adjusted his position. More sand gathered on the towel. Maybe Sam was right about the yoga mat. The sand was becoming a problem, and in this weird position, it was creeping into places he didn't want to think about. And how could Sam bend into those positions? She was right about one thing, though, the view was great... of *her*.

Why had she invited him to sit here? Wasn't yoga supposed to be solitary, like meditation? And why was she asking him all these questions? It was like an interrogation, and she wasn't very good at it, either, not like Cole. He was a pro. But if she was going to interrogate him, he could do the same. "I know you're a lawyer and all, but didn't you ever want to get into the family business?"

Cole had been wondering about that. Who wouldn't want to run a family business that had been handed down over generations? And he could tell by her clothing and the budget rental car model that she wasn't exactly rolling in the dough, so money couldn't be the motivation for her lawyering. He could only conclude that they needed money to keep the business going.

"I just never wanted to stay in this small town. It

didn't seem very ambitious to just fall into a family business when I was younger."

Something in her voice gave him pause. Did he sense a tone of longing and regret, a feeling that maybe she'd made the wrong choice? He glanced over to see a pensive look on her face. He felt an unwanted bond, thinking they might be in the same position, questioning their career choices. He pushed the feeling away. He wasn't here to make friends. He was here to save his dad.

"Well, it's good your mom is improving the business now. Seems like it'll pay off." Cole was probing to find out about the money part of it, trying to get Sam to say she couldn't have afforded it before.

But she didn't say anything. She simply sat cross-legged on her mat, bowed her head, and mumbled some woo-woo word.

She stood and started rolling up her yoga mat. "Well, have a good meditation."

He watched her walk off. Darn! He hadn't gotten in all the questions he wanted to, but that was okay. He had some other ideas up his sleeve on how to prove Deena and Sam were up to something.

He adjusted his position. This meditation thing was a lot harder than the therapist had made it sound. Maybe a yoga mat would help.

He glanced down the beach, his thoughts turning to the fugitive Gary had sent a picture of. The picture was pretty grainy, but Cole thought he would recognize the person even though their face was partially covered by the hoodie they were wearing. And with this summer weather and beautiful scenery, he knew exactly what he would do if he were a fugitive in town. He'd camp out right on the beach.

To the north, the beach was isolated, not a house or building in sight. No people lounging around indicated there was no beach access, either. It was a perfect place for someone running from the law to make camp.

Gina cradled the phone between her shoulder and her ear as she reached up in the cabinet for a large canister of pastry flour. Ellie was on the other end of the phone and had just informed her that she'd located Holly. Bad news, Hugh was nowhere to be found.

"I don't understand. Where would Hugh go?" Gina asked.

Did they break up? Maybe Holly did away with him, not that Gina would blame her, but she hoped that wasn't the case because she needed Hugh to get her money.

"I have no idea, but don't worry. I'm going to find out. In the meantime, though, there's an interesting development. I have a friend in the FBI, and rumor is there's an agent in town."

"Here in Shell Cove? Looking for Hugh?" Gina reached for the sugar canister.

"I don't know. I think it could be the person that was looking for *you*."

"Me?" Gina opened a drawer and absently rooted for the measuring cups, her mind trying to grapple with why the FBI would be looking for her.

Gina sensed hesitation on the other end of phone, and then Ellie said, "Look, I have to ask you something, but please don't get offended."

Gina pulled out the measuring cups and put them next to the canisters on the counter. "Okay." She drew the word out.

"Is there any way that the authorities might think you were involved in whatever Hugh was into?"

"Me? No way! I had no idea what was going on."

"I believe you. But Hugh and Holly are kind of shady. Maybe there is something that points to you and you just don't know it. They could have finagled things on the way out to cast blame on you."

Gina's blood chilled. Could there be something implicating her? But after Hugh and Holly had disappeared, the police had gone over all their accounts. Everything in their office had been seized, computer records, bank accounts, customer files. At first, they had questioned her aggressively, but it soon became clear that she had nothing to do with any criminal activity, and they'd let up on their questions.

Except... there was one document the police hadn't seen, the one she'd found in Hugh's office safe. And that document was sitting at the bank in her safety deposit box.

"I don't think there is anything. The police have already gone over everything from the office."

But what if there was something in that document? Gina hadn't looked it over thoroughly, and what she'd seen, she didn't really understand. She'd just known that its presence in Hugh's home office safe meant it was important. Why hadn't he taken it with him? Had he left it because it was some fake document that implicated her? Perhaps she'd better scrutinize it further. If there was something that somehow implicated her, she'd have to destroy it, and if that were the case, that meant she really had no leverage to get her money from Hugh.

"Okay. Maybe the FBI is here for some other reason. Or my information could be wrong. Sometimes, these clandestine tips don't pan out."

"Right," Gina said.

"Okay, well, I'll keep searching for Hugh. I still have some avenues to follow. I'll keep you updated."

She disconnected from Ellie. It was only noon. She had plenty of time to get to the bank, but she didn't want to wait. She swooped the ingredients up from the counter and shoved them in the cabinet then ripped off her apron and headed toward the lobby door.

But before she made it halfway through the lobby, the door opened, and an elderly couple came in.

"Hi, we're the Bradfords, and we're checking in today."

Crap! This was just what she didn't need. But Gina couldn't be rude, so she pasted on her best customer-servicing smile, slipped behind the counter, and checked them in.

She tried to be cordial and not rush, taking the time to answer all of their questions thoroughly. Hopefully, they hadn't seen her eyes continuously darting to the clock on the wall.

Finally, they left for their room, and she made a beeline for the door again.

But before she reached it, Jules bounced in. Her face was flushed, and she looked like she was in a hurry. Seriously, now of all times? Jules had been with Nick for a few days, and if she had only just stayed away for another few minutes, Gina would have been well on her way to the bank.

"I'm so sorry I left you here all alone! But I'm back now, and I'll be here for the next several days straight. You should take some days off. I'll watch the motel." Jules really did look sorry about leaving the motel in Gina's hands, but Gina didn't mind.

"It's no problem. I don't have anywhere else to go, and I'm here baking pies anyway." Would it be rude to dart out the door when Jules had just arrived?

"Oh, by the way, did you notice all those footprints in the mulch around the motel?" Jules asked. "Someone trampled the petunias and the impatiens! Was it one of the guests?"

Gina stopped short. She'd thought the impatiens under the window sill had been trampled, but she hadn't looked any further. She could see an animal trying to get at the pie, but why would it go all around the motel? "Really? All around?"

"Yeah. Kinda weird. Maybe a raccoon or something?" Jules asked. "I think Maddie was onto something, though, with being worried about you being here alone. You won't be alone the next few days since I'll be here, but I think we should start locking the door. Nick is coming over too. You don't mind, do you? The bank is closing early today and won't open again until Tuesday in honor of the town anniversary."

Gina stared at Jules. "The bank is closing? When?"

"Noon." Jules glanced at her wrist. "Oh! Looks like it's closed already. Nick should be here any minute, then."

Shoot! Gina had missed her chance to go to the bank, and it was going to be closed until Tuesday. Now what was she going to do?

CHAPTER 12

The air at Saltwater Sweets was thick with the scent of chocolate. Sam dipped a maple cream center in thick velvety liquid and swirled it around to get it evenly coated. Fond memories of making chocolates with her mother and grandmother bubbled up.

As a child, she'd delighted in taking part in the candy-making process. Her mother had let her try her hand at everything: fudge, bark, caramels. But making the cream-center chocolates was her favorite.

Once she'd gotten to her teenage years, other things had taken precedence over making candy. In high school, she'd decided that working in the family business was the lamest thing ever. All her friends had set their sights on big and important careers, journalism, acting, medicine. She wanted a career like that, too, so she chose law.

She'd achieved her goal on that one, but now she was discovering that things weren't always as exciting as you thought they were going to be. She glanced down at the chocolates all lined up in a row. There was a certain satisfaction in the simple task of creating something with your hands that she just didn't get from her job as an attorney.

It was good to spend time alone with her mother. They were close and talked at least twice a week, but there was nothing like catching up in person. Now, if only Deena would stop gushing about Chuck.

"When Chuck first asked me out, I had no idea what to do. I mean, I hadn't dated anyone but your father, and that was when I was nineteen!" Deena chuckled as she cut a block of penuche fudge.

"I'm glad you were able to get out of your comfort zone." Sam couldn't think of anything else positive to say. She didn't want to encourage her mother's feelings for Chuck, but Deena seemed so happy that she didn't know how to broach the topic that he might not be what he seemed.

"But what really got me was that charming dimple when he smiles." Deena sighed, a goofy smile on her face.

Cole had that dimple, too, except his wasn't charming.

"It's nice that he helps out here, but maybe he's doing too much. It sounds like he's taken over the websites and he's rearranged the entire store." Sam gestured to the racks. "I mean, it's not like he has a stake in the business."

Deena looked up and frowned at her daughter. "A stake?"

"Yeah, you know, like part ownership." Sam was fishing, and if Chuck was doing something fishy, hopefully her questions would shake something loose.

"Oh? Do you think it's unfair? Maybe he should have a stake. I mean, he has done a lot."

Okay, well, that backfired, but Sam could use it to dig deeper. "Is that what he thinks? Has he mentioned anything about getting more ownership of Saltwater Sweets?"

Deena appeared confused. "No. Well, he has mentioned something about the bank accounts, but that's only so that he could invest some money."

Ha! So he *was* up to something! Of course, he was letting Deena think it was so that he could invest money, but Sam bet it was the opposite.

Sam focused on the chocolate making while she contemplated the best way to get her mother to see what was clearly obvious about Chuck's intentions.

The work was soothingly repetitive, almost like a meditation, and she let her gaze wander around the shop, her eyes falling on the old picture she'd noticed earlier. "Is that a new picture there?" Sam jutted her chin toward it.

"Yes. That's Etta Harper, your great-great-grandmother. I told you about her, right?"

"Of course. I recognized that it was taken here in the shop. Looks funny without much in it."

"I know. And that one next to it is her in Starfish Cottage. You know that old cottage down on the beach that was falling apart?"

"Yeah, I think I remember it. Didn't it used to be a rental?" Sam vaguely remembered going to a party there when she was a teenager.

Deena nodded. "Yep. Then it fell into disrepair. Anyway, one of the girls that bought the Beachcomber Motel bought it and was renovating it. Turns out she discovered Etta Harper had ties to that cottage. She found an old recipe for whiskey fudge in the drawer. Isn't that a hoot?"

"It sure is. I don't remember anyone talking about the cottage being in the family."

Her mother looked up from her task of making the swirls, a mischievous gleam in her eye. "That's because no one wanted anyone to know. It has a shady past. Seems that it was associated with the bootlegger."

Sam glanced at the photo. "So our relative was in cahoots with the bootlegger?"

Her mother laughed. "Seems so."

That was actually kind of interesting. Maybe her family business wasn't as boring as she'd always thought. Sam felt an unusual nostalgia for her family and the business bubbling up.

She'd always looked at the business as something she *had* to do, something that was expected of her, not something that she wanted to do.

Running a small business in a small town had seemed so unambitious. But now that she was older, she was starting to see things differently, especially since the shine had worn off her lawyer job in the city. For the first time ever, she could actually envision herself working in Saltwater Sweets alongside her mother, satisfied to make the best chocolates on the East Coast.

She was afraid there wouldn't be any store for her to work in if she couldn't figure out what Chuck was up to. Her mom was deeply infatuated with the man, and Sam knew she would need solid proof in order for her mother to see the truth. Since he'd been working on changing things on the computer, perhaps she would find that proof there.

"Potty break." Sam stripped off her gloves and headed to the back.

The little office was across from the bathroom, and Sam looked back over her shoulder to make sure her mother was out of sight before slipping into the office instead of the bathroom.

She rushed over to the computer, surprised to discover that the password was still the same. It was weird that Chuck hadn't changed it. A quick search didn't yield any sinister results. The software looked legit, and a glance at the company bank accounts seemed fine. Whatever Chuck was up to would take some more digging.

She pulled the keyboard closer and noticed a wallet behind the monitor. Chuck's?

Ellie had said she used a database that keyed off

Social Security numbers, so maybe Sam could get access to that database too. Her dad always carried his Social Security card in his wallet… did Chuck?

Before she even realized what she was doing, she'd grabbed the wallet and rushed over to the table by the back door, where she'd thrown her purse. She could quickly dig out her phone and take a picture of the Social Security number, and no one would be the wiser.

She reached into her purse, her fingers brushing the hard plastic of the phone case, and then—

"I forgot to tell you the toilet is acting weird!"

Oh no, her mother was coming down the hallway.

It was too late to put the wallet back on the desk. Deena was almost at the door and might see her. Sam did the only thing she could think of and shoved the wallet into her purse.

Her mom appeared in the doorway, looking confused to see Sam standing there. "Oh, you were taking so long in the bathroom I was wondering if the toilet was acting up again. Sometimes you have to jiggle the handle."

"Oh no. It was fine. I just was getting a lipstick out of my purse." Sam reached in, pulled out a lipstick, and smeared it on her lips as if to prove her point.

"Oh. Okay. That's a pretty color, dear." Deena glanced at the computer, and Sam's heart lurched as she wondered if her mother knew somehow she'd been on it. Maybe she'd notice the keyboard was in a different place. But then her mother gave her her usual loving smile and said, "Are you ready to make more chocolates? I'm doing some white peppermint bark to bring to the celebration as well."

Sam followed her out to the front of the shop. The idea of making more chocolates was a welcome one, except now it was marred with guilt and worry. How in the world was she going to return Chuck's wallet before he noticed it was missing?

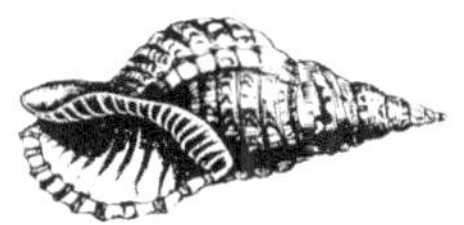

CHAPTER 13

Cole peered through the curtains in the motel room window into the parking lot. Sam's car was gone from its usual spot. Good. He was looking forward to a day of golfing with his dad, without the interference of Sam and her mother.

"I think your imagination is working overtime." His sister, Audrey's, voice sounded amused on the other end of the phone. "Deena is perfectly nice and makes Dad happy. He deserves to be happy."

"I want Dad to be happy, but I'm telling you this Deena lady is up to something." Cole was sure of it.

"Seriously?" His sister sounded exasperated. "Do you have some proof of that?"

"She has him making chocolates, and I think he's considering buying expensive equipment for the business." Cole frowned at his own words. That didn't seem like very much proof.

"Let me remind you that Dad is a grown man and

can make his own decisions. I highly doubt he's going to appreciate you butting in, and besides, you're damaged from your job. Maybe you aren't assessing the situation correctly. Just enjoy the vacation. It wouldn't be a bad idea for you to follow Dad's lead and meet a woman too."

Visions of Sam immediately sprang to mind, and Cole's frown deepened. He'd sworn off women after the last breakup, but the truth was he was kind of lonely. He wanted someone to share his life with. Not Sam, though. Even though she was attractive, she was clearly shady.

He turned his mind back to saving his father. "But Dad is so nice and easily taken advantage of. Plus, he has a lot of money, which makes him a target."

"He can handle himself. Besides, it gives him joy to help people. Remember how he helped our old cleaning lady, Mrs. Newcomb, establish her new business?"

Cole pulled a golf shirt out of the closet and laid it on the bed. "Yeah, but he invested money in that and got a good return. That was a business deal. And he wasn't all googly-eyed over Mrs. Newcomb. He's not getting any money back from Saltwater Sweets, and I doubt there's any kind of contract there."

"But Dad didn't help Mrs. Newcomb for the money. He did it to help a nice person succeed. The money was only a byproduct, and if Dad wants to just help Deena, then we should let him. It's his money, not ours."

"I suppose." Audrey did have a point. His father was a grown man and could make his own decisions about how he spent his money. Cole wasn't expecting any inheritance. Quite the opposite. He wanted his dad to enjoy his money while he could. And Cole certainly hadn't liked it when his dad had butted into his life.

"All I'm saying is just try to give her the benefit of the doubt. If you relax and enjoy yourself, you might find you have a good time. You're not exactly in a good frame of mind to be making judgements on people right now." Audrey's voice held a tinge of worry, and Cole felt bad that his sister might be worrying about him. "I'm coming out in a few weeks to see for myself. I'm sure Deena is delightful."

Cole snorted. Despite what Audrey said about his frame of mind, Cole trusted his own judgement, and if he had anything to say about it, Deena would be out of the picture long before Audrey came out to visit their dad.

Cole planted his feet shoulder width apart and lined his club up against the golf ball. He pulled back then swung forward and watched the ball sail through the blue sky.

He shaded his eyes. Come on… a little more to the left. But the ball kept going to the right. His shoulders slumped as it started to drop.

Splash! Right into the pond.

"You seem a little distracted, son," Chuck said. "Is it about your job?"

Cole hadn't told his father the details of what had happened on his job. His dad knew that he worked undercover for the FBI on kidnapping cases and the job was emotionally intense. Saving victims of kidnapping crimes didn't always have a good result. This last case had involved twins, one of whom hadn't made it, and it weighed heavily on Cole. But that wasn't something he liked to burden anyone else with, least of all his father.

"No, things are fine. I'm feeling a lot better about it."

Chuck stared at him for a while. "It's Deena, then. I noticed that you haven't warmed to her."

The disappointment in his father's voice stung and made him feel like a jerk. But also, he couldn't just let his dad be taken advantage of, though he knew he needed to tread carefully on that subject.

He remained silent while his dad took his shot.

"Nice one!" Cole said. Unlike his own shot, Chuck's had landed within feet of the hole. It would be an easy putt in.

"I'm sure Deena is very nice, but maybe you are rushing into things."

"At our age, we can't take too long. Besides, when you know someone is right, you know." Chuck started toward the hole.

"Still, she has you doing a lot at the candy store. I thought you liked being retired."

"I like being with Deena, and if that means working in the candy store, I'm happy to do it." Chuck nodded toward the edge of the green where Cole's ball had crossed into the pond. "You can drop a ball and take your shot."

Cole took the shot, this time getting right up to the hole. It was a one-stroke penalty anyway, and his dad was so far ahead he'd never win. But this game wasn't about winning, to Cole. It was about making his dad see Deena a little differently.

"Is this about your mother?" Chuck asked as he lined up his shot. "Your mom isn't here anymore—Lord knows I wish she was—and no one can replace her, but what I have with Deena is independent of that. It's just as wonderful but different."

Cole was getting a little frustrated. His dad wasn't reading between the lines. He might have to be blunter. "Don't you think it's a little weird that her daughter showed up at the same time I did?"

Chuck gave him a questioning look. "What do you mean?"

"Well, you must've told Deena when I was coming, and then she invited Sam to come during the same week. Maybe that's because she was worried I might see something in her that you don't. She figured Sam could create a distraction. I mean, you are quite wealthy, and…" Cole let the sentence trail off.

Chuck shook his head, and Cole could see the disappointment in his father's expression. Unfortunately, it wasn't disappointment in Deena, as he'd hoped. It was disappointment in Cole for his negative thoughts. "There's nothing different to see, son. Deena's not after my money. She has no idea how much I have. And

Sam's presence in town didn't happen exactly like that. We wanted you both to come, and this happened to be the time that you both had off."

Cole nodded, but he could tell by the way his dad was rubbing his chin that he might have hit a nerve. Guilt washed over him at the look of sadness suddenly in his father's expression. Could he be wrong about Deena?

"Sorry, Dad. I didn't mean to doubt Deena's intentions, but you're a nice guy, and I don't want you to be taken advantage of."

"I appreciate that." Chuck's eyes were on the ball as he putted it right into the hole and gestured for Cole to take his turn.

Cole sank his ball then turned to his father. He felt bad for all the discouraging talk about Deena and wanted to lighten the mood.

"Deena does seem very nice, and it's good for you to have something to do. The chocolates are delicious too." He clapped his dad on the back. "Come on. Let's finish this round, then lunch is on me."

Chuck laughed. "It's going to have to be. I think I left my wallet at Saltwater Sweets. Why do you think I let you pay for this round of golf?"

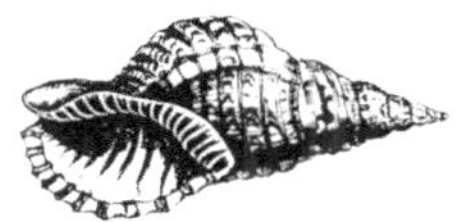

CHAPTER 14

Chuck arrived at Deena's small apartment that night with a bottle of wine, a bouquet of roses, and a few doubts that he hadn't had before his round of golf with Cole.

When they'd agreed to meet up after their day alone with their children, Chuck had envisioned showing up full of relief that Cole was warming to her and approved of their relationship. He was hoping Deena would say the same about Sam. He hated to admit that Cole had planted some doubts about Deena's intentions, and now they were swirling in his brain like buzzards.

Surely, his son's reservations were ridiculous. Cole was used to thinking people had the worst intentions because of his job. That's all it was. Deena and Sam weren't up to anything. Deena had never asked him for a penny or forced him to help her. He'd volunteered. Or at least that was the way he remembered it.

"Roses? How sweet!" The look of joy and innocence on Deena's face washed any doubts away.

He kissed her on the cheek. "How was your day with Sam?"

"Fabulous." He followed her into the kitchen, where she laid the roses on the counter and pulled two trays out of the fridge. "We made these white-chocolate-covered strawberries, peppermint bark, assorted chocolates, and even lollipops for the kids."

Chuck surveyed the trays, where everything was lined up in neat rows. The bark was cut into perfectly sized chunks, the chocolates glistening, the lollipops dipped in sprinkles. He imagined the chocolate melting all over the kids' faces in the hot sun, the children laughing as parents ran after them with wet wipes.

"Sam used to love making chocolates when she was a little girl, but as she got older, she kind of drifted away." A look of sadness crossed Deena's face, but then she brightened. "But I felt like something happened today, like she started to appreciate the business more. I know it's silly, but maybe she'll even think about coming back to Shell Cove."

Chuck was grateful that at least Sam hadn't instilled the same doubts about him that Cole had about Deena.

Deena put the chocolates back in the fridge, took a cut-crystal vase out of the cabinet, and started arranging the roses.

"It's great that both our kids could be here the same week. Though maybe it would have been better if they came on separate weeks. That way, we could have spent more time with each one individually. Maybe we should have coordinated better." Guilty feelings swarmed. Hopefully, Deena wouldn't think that Chuck was fishing for information. Despite what he'd told Cole, he couldn't remember if they'd discussed when their kids would come or not.

"Yeah, maybe. But it's kind of nice that they are getting to know each other. Just a coincidence they could come the same week. I do wish Audrey could be here to meet Sam too." Deena's tone was light as she stepped back to survey the rose arrangement.

Chuck was relieved. Deena hadn't planned for Sam to come on the same week. It was just an innocent coincidence. Her mention of Audrey reminded Chuck that his daughter didn't share Cole's reservations.

"How was your day with Cole, dear?" Deena looked at him with hopeful, optimistic eyes. He wouldn't dream of mentioning Cole's suspicions to her.

"It was great. It's been a while since we were able to get in a round of golf. Cole is so busy with his job and all." Chuck had told Deena briefly about Cole's job and that he had just come off a big case. "Speaking of which, have you seen my wallet? It's a sentimental piece that Cole gave me and has a trout on the front. I discovered I didn't have it when we golfed, and Cole had to pay for the golf and lunch."

Deena laughed. "I'm sure he didn't mind. He's a grown man with his own money, and sometimes kids like to treat."

Chuck stiffened. Was that a weird thing to say?

Cole's words about Chuck having a lot of money and insinuating that Deena might be after it raced through his mind. Was she glad Cole paid for golf and lunch so that Chuck would have more money for her? She'd never mentioned money before.

Deena put the roses on the small kitchen table beside the window. "I haven't seen it, but you usually put it on the desk in the office at Saltwater Sweets when you are working on the computer, don't you? You said it's uncomfortable to sit on."

"That's right. I must've left it there. I was a little distracted with the golfing and was trying to rush the day's receipts into the system. I'll look for it tomorrow before the town celebration."

Deena's smile faltered. "I am a little worried about the celebration. I hope spending the whole day with Cole and Sam isn't going to be too forced. I'm still worried that Cole doesn't like me."

Deena looked so sad that Chuck instinctively gave her a hug. "Don't worry about that. Cole was devastated when Angie died. They were very close. And even though it has been years, he probably needs some time to get used to the idea of me being with another woman. He held her out at arm's length, his hands on her shoulders. You're the first I've dated… and hopefully the last."

"That's so sweet." Deena's look of love melted his heart and vanquished any doubts he had about her.

"But to tell you the truth, I have the same concerns

about Sam. I'm afraid I might have hurt her feelings by doing the work on the computer."

Deena shook her head. "I don't know why, because Sam has never been interested in doing the computer work at Saltwater Sweets. But I suppose she might need some time to get used to the idea of us being together for the same reasons. She was close with her dad."

Chuck nodded. "All the more reason to make sure they see how happy we are tomorrow. Don't worry. I know we can win them over. And we have the added surprise that will really bring all of us together."

CHAPTER 15

The town common, with its wide grassy area bordered by tall oak, maple, and pine trees, was bustling with activity when Gina arrived with her pies tucked into two triple-tier carriers the next day.

The tables were already loaded with dozens of homemade dishes. Those that needed to be kept chilled were set atop trays filled with ice. A few feet from the tables, several large charcoal grills sizzled and smoked, spicing the air with the mouthwatering smell of grilled meat.

On the other side of the common, games had been set up: horseshoes, cornhole, and badminton. Kids were running around, and adults were mingling. Gina found herself smiling at the festive mood.

"You brought so many!" Maddie exclaimed as she helped her unload the pies on one of the dessert tables.

Jules pitched in, too, putting the little mesh dome covers that Gina had brought over each one. Had she gone overboard by bringing six? Many people in town had brought dishes, and there were more than enough desserts for everyone. But she loved making them and wanted a variety.

"The apple is my favorite." Dex eyed the apple pie with its perfectly browned crust glittering with sugar crystals.

"Keep your hands off until dessert!" Maddie nudged him good-naturedly.

"I like the chocolate cream." Nick reached for the pie, earning an elbow to the ribs from Jules.

He laughed. "Seriously, Gina, you should go into business making these. I'd be happy to try to push a business loan through."

Nick worked at the Shell Cove bank and had gotten them a loan for the Beachcomber. Maybe she'd have to resort to that, but she was really hoping not to get into debt. Though with the chances of finding Hugh diminishing, she might have to resort to borrowing money.

"Yeah, you should think about opening a shop." Belinda Simms, from the town hall, had come up and was looking over the pies. "Best pies ever."

"We could use a pie shop in town." Cassie Fox, from Ocean Brew, wiggled her brows. "Just sayin'."

"Remember what I said about your future," Maddie reminded her.

Gina felt embarrassed with all the attention on her. "I do like making pies, but enough about me. I have to tell you everything looks great. You pulled off another fantastic event, cuz."

Maddie's smile widened. "Thanks. I like doing it."

Dex put his arm around her shoulders. "She's great at putting events together, isn't she?"

"She is." Gina refrained from making a face as the two exchanged adoring looks. She was happy that both of her cousins had found love, but she hoped theirs didn't end up like Gina's had. That probably wouldn't happen. Nick and Dex weren't jerks like Hugh.

"Oh look, there's Rose, Leena, and Pearl." Maddie waved at the three ladies.

Gina was glad when they started over toward them. She hadn't seen the welcome wagon ladies in a few days, and at least she wouldn't feel like a fifth wheel standing here with the two happy couples.

Rose's heart swelled at the way Dex rushed over to give her a kiss on the cheek and take the potato salad bowl from her. He was such a sweet young man. Well, maybe not so *young*, he was over thirty, but Rose still thought of him as a boy.

She was surprised he'd torn himself away from Maddie's side. The two had been inseparable lately, and she couldn't be more pleased.

"Thank you, dear." Rose watched as Dex put the salad in one of the cooling trays and then returned to Maddie's side.

"What did you two bring?" Rose asked them.

"Macaroni salad just like you showed me." Maddie beamed as she gestured toward a colorful bowl.

Rose had spent the previous afternoon with Maddie, showing her different variations of macaroni salad. You'd think macaroni salad would be simple, but Rose knew a few tricks: different spices to put in the mayonnaise, different additions like hot dogs—which the little kids loved—and tomatoes, which could only be added at the last minute. It had been a joy to spend time alone with Maddie, and Rose could see why Dex was so smitten. Maddie was so smart and picked things up quickly. She was exactly what her grandson needed.

"Are these your pies, Gina?" Pearl turned from the dessert table to look at Gina, her left eyebrow raised.

"Yes. I may have overdone it. I brought six." Gina shrugged.

Pearl laughed. "People are usually clamoring for more. I bet they won't last but a few hours."

Rose saw a look pass between Gina and Pearl as if they had some sort of secret. If they did, Rose had no idea what it was. That was okay. Everyone had secrets, and Rose suspected Gina had more than one.

"I even brought something homemade this time," Jules piped in.

"You did?" Rose remembered the first town meeting the three cousins had been invited to, when they'd brought some god-awful dipped-fruit dish. Subsequent meetings had shown that their cooking skills had not improved, until now, apparently.

Jules rushed over to the dessert table and picked up

a plate piled high with large cookies. "Chocolate chip cookies."

Nick leaned in toward them. "I actually was the one who baked them."

"Stop! Don't give away my secrets!" Jules swatted at him playfully.

"Hey ho!" A vivacious senior citizen with red hair and a flowing hot-pink caftan fluttered up to the table.

Aggie Fletcher was a fun addition to town. Rose, Leena, and Pearl had had coffee with her a few times and even cut her in on one of their bets. She liked the way Aggie had brightened the outlook of their old friend Henry Barlowe, who was hurrying along in her wake.

"I brought pickled cucumbers. It's my specialty." Aggie set the dish down, and a round of greetings and hugs ensued.

"Hey, Gramps!" Nick hugged his grandfather. The two were still as close as they had been when he was a little boy.

Rose scanned the crowd as they talked about the various festivities of the day. It was a good turnout, and the mood was festive. Quite a difference from the somber town mood of last summer. Things were really looking up in Shell Cove.

At least, it was looking up for some of them. Rose's gaze stopped at four people standing over by the bandstand. She dug her elbow into Leena's side. "Look, there's Deena, Chuck, and their children. Let's go over and say hi."

Leena followed her gaze, her eyes narrowing. "Things look a little awkward. We better get over there."

They caught Pearl's attention, said their goodbyes, and hurried over. They had promised Deena and Chuck they would help make a big deal out of how the two were perfect for each other in front of Sam and Cole, and it looked like there was no better time than now to make good on that promise.

Cole was actually enjoying the small-town vibe of the Shell Cove two-hundred-fifty-year celebration. The guys back at the office would have gotten a kick out of that.

It was hard not to feel upbeat, though, when everyone seemed so happy. And the grassy town common was laid out with balloons and streamers. The various food dishes made it seem more like a gigantic family picnic than an organized town celebration. Kids ran through the crowd giggling, couples strolled hand in hand, and everyone seemed to be enjoying themselves.

Even Sam seemed to be a bit lighter today. Her shoulders were more relaxed, and her hair drawn up atop her head made her look like she was a teenager. And her crisp daisy-pattern dress was loose and flowy but somehow managed to hug her curves in a way that was innocent and sexy at the same time. She was giving off a total girl-next-door vibe, which Cole found a bit distracting.

Had the girl-next-door thing been done on purpose to try to make him forget any suspicions he had? No one could be that calculating. As Audrey had said, Cole was letting his imagination and his suspicious nature get the best of him.

Today, he was going to put his suspicions on the back burner and enjoy himself. He knew his father had been disappointed to hear his concerns about Deena, and he didn't want to ruin the day for his dad. What if Audrey was right, and he was making too much out of it? He should back off and let his father make his own decisions.

Plus, it seemed like Deena was really trying. She was being very nice and had even gone out of her way to make his favorite seven-layer dip in addition to all the chocolates.

Cole suspected his father had told her that his mother usually made that dip for him. He could see how eager she was for his approval, so he made a big deal about it, dipping a chip in and gushing about how delicious it was.

Cole had more pressing matters on his mind than his father's romance, anyway. His attempt at morning meditation had failed, but when he'd taken a walk down the beach, he'd hit pay dirt. A pile of burned driftwood indicated someone had been camping on a remote part of the beach just out of sight of any houses. He also found some tuna cans in the dunes.

"Oh! Here come Rose, Leena, and Pearl." Sam seemed overly excited about the three senior citizens approaching them.

Clearly, everyone except Cole knew them. They exchanged a greeting, and then his dad introduced him.

"It's so great to finally meet you," the tallest one, named Rose, said. "Your dad speaks very highly of you."

Cole felt a swell of pride and smiled at his dad.

"We're so grateful that your dad came to town and put the spark in Deena's eyes again," Lena said.

"They seem happy." Cole glanced at his father and Deena, who were staring at him with overeager looks on their faces.

"Oh, very happy. And they're just such a great couple. So perfect for each other." Pearl leaned in to accent the word *perfect*.

Cole's brow furrowed. It seemed like these ladies were laying it on a little too thick. He glanced at Deena again. Had she put them up to it? Were the three ladies in on her and Sam's plan?

But before he had a chance to think too much about it, his father clapped his hands. "Look, there's an opening at one of the cornhole boards!" Chuck pointed to their left, where several cornhole games had been set up in a row. "Deena and I would like to challenge you and Sam to a game. Come on!"

Team up with Sam? Cole wasn't so sure about that. But it was too late, his father was already halfway over to the game, so he shrugged and followed. He was here all day. Might as well make the best of it.

Sam held her breath as she watched the beanbag sail through the air and right through the hole on the cornhole board. "Score!"

She jumped up in the air, spun around, and high-fived Cole.

Whoa, wait a minute. When had they become so chummy? Had that actually happened just over the span of the afternoon?

Apparently, somehow it had. Maybe it was the festive air of the celebration or the fact that her mother and Chuck looked so pleased to be doing this simple activity with them. Somehow, over the five games of cornhole, the food tasting, and the parade, she and Cole had formed—if not a bond—at least some sort of a truce.

Guilt washed over her, and she turned away, pretending to scan the crowd and thinking about Chuck's wallet, which sat in a drawer in her motel room. She hadn't had a chance to sneak into Saltwater Sweets yet to return it.

The day had given her a chance to study Chuck and her mother together. He treated her mother like a queen, and he was polite, considerate, and sweet to both of them, not the gruff, domineering opportunist she'd imagined. Had her job jaded her so much that she'd just jumped to assuming the worst for no real reason?

"Don't get too cocky." Chuck swung his beanbag back and forth as he took aim. "We're still ahead."

He tossed the bag, which landed on the board and then slid into the hole.

"Darn!" Cole handed Sam the next bag. "Come on. You can do it. We can still beat them if you get a hole in one."

No pressure there. Sam planted her feet and grabbed the bag by the corner. She held the bag up in front of her like a bowler aiming for the middle pin and concentrated on the hole at the top of the board. She took a few swings and then let go.

Plop.

Ugh, it landed on the edge of the board and then fell off.

"Guess that's it. We won the championship!" Chuck said.

Deena jumped up and down, clapping her hands, and then she and Chuck hugged. He gave her the sweetest kiss on the cheek, and Sam noticed that look again. It was a look of pure love. Surely, he couldn't be *that* good of an actor.

"Don't get so excited. We let you win." Cole winked at Sam. "Didn't we, Sam?"

"Yes. Absolutely."

Deena and Chuck came over to their side, and there were handshakes all around.

"You know, this has been so much fun. I've enjoyed

spending time with all of us together." Chuck's tone was sincere.

"Me too. I really don't want the day to end." Sam was surprised to find that she really felt that way.

"Well, that's good." Deena slipped her arm through Sam's, excitement evident on her face. "Because Chuck and I have a little surprise that's going to extend the day, and we think you guys are really going to like it."

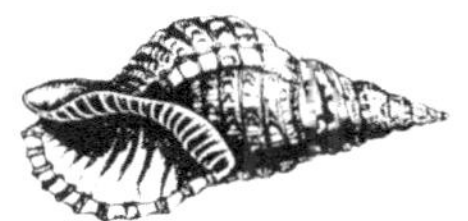

CHAPTER 16

Gina had left the town celebration while it was in midswing. She wandered along Main Street, making a point to go past the vacant bakery on her way to her car. The shop was still empty, and she lingered at the window, imagining the tables and chairs set up and filled with happy pie-eating customers.

The bakery cases looked almost new and she pictured those filled with various pies. The blackboard behind the counter would have the specials written in colorful chalk. She'd already come up with some unique items like small individual-sized pies and pies filled with savory ingredients for lunch.

She still had no word on Hugh. How long should she wait? Nick had sounded upbeat about her getting a loan. Maddie, Jules, and she were taking only a small salary from the Beachcomber motel profits, choosing to put everything back into the motel, and she didn't have anything saved up. Maybe she should just forget about Hugh and apply. Avoiding debt was the best course of action, though, so she would wait a little longer.

When she got back to the Beachcomber, it was quiet. Everyone was at the town celebration. She was cleaning up the last-minute pie-baking mess in the motel kitchen when she heard a strange noise out by the porch.

It sounded like something big. Could it be the animal that had been nibbling her pie crusts?

If it was, then she wanted to discourage it from coming around. She scuttled out the kitchen door and started cautiously toward the front of the motel.

She heard more noise, possibly coming from the crawl space under the porch. It was covered with lattice, but the hinge on the little door was broken, and she supposed an animal could have pushed it open.

Hmm, maybe she should get some sort of weapon in case it came at her. She grabbed a piece of driftwood they'd placed as a decoration in the garden and tiptoed toward the front.

She had no intention of going in there after it, but maybe she could scare it out. She didn't want it thinking the area under the porch was a good place to make a nest or den.

She paused when she got to the front. Something was definitely in there, rummaging around. Maybe she should call the police. They were all at the celebration, though, and this thing might do some damage before they could get here.

She raised the driftwood over her head. "Scat! Get out! Shoo!"

Something backed out the door.

Gina dropped the driftwood, frozen in shock.

"Hugh, is that you?"

CHAPTER 17

The sailboat was an old classic with crisp white paint and polished teak trim. It was different from the one Cole and his parents had had when he was younger, but it still brought a flood of childhood memories.

The look of pride on his father's face as he explained how he'd restored the boat was worth the trip to see it. The sunset cruise was a bonus that Cole hadn't expected.

Deena and Sam had proven to be worthy sailors, and the four of them had worked as a team to get the boat offshore. Now, they were sailing through the choppy waters with the wind in their hair and smiles on their faces, like old friends or maybe even… family.

"I guess a sailor never forgets his tricks," Chuck said as they perched on the windward side of the boat. He reached into a small cooler and pulled out a six-pack of beer and offered them each one. To his surprise, both

Deena and Sam seemed delighted. He would have pegged them for wine drinkers.

"That's true." Deena snugged down her baseball cap. "Though the first few times we took this out were a little nerve-racking."

"How many times have you been out?" Sam shaded her eyes as she squinted into the setting sun to look at her mother.

"Just a couple of times. Chuck only finished it last month." Deena beamed at Chuck proudly.

Cole realized his dad had been living a whole other life here, and it included more than just making chocolates. He seemed happy.

Chuck tore his gaze from Deena and held his beer can up. "Well, here's to teamwork." He tipped his beer forward, and they all clinked.

Cole's eyes met Sam's and lingered. Yesterday, he would've laughed if you'd said that he and Sam had been part of the same team, but today, it seemed totally natural. And he felt the bond that had loosely formed during the cornhole game tighten just a little bit.

Sam laughed as a cold blast of sea spray hit her in the face. It was exhilarating to be out sailing again.

To the west, the sun kissed the ocean, lighting the sky with hues of gold and pink. The breeze whipped her hair, and she felt freer than she had in years.

She'd been so busy holed up in her office, going over

legal documents and meeting clients, that she hadn't enjoyed any activity like this in ages. Why hadn't she ever made the time before?

She could tell by the looks her mother and Chuck were giving each other that they were happy with the way the day had turned out. It was great that Chuck had restored this boat, and clearly, her mother enjoyed having it. It was something they could do together, but a little part of her wondered how he'd paid for it. Had it been all his money, or had Deena chipped in? It was none of her business, though, and why shouldn't her mother have chipped in if she enjoyed it too?

"You know, you and Cole have a lot more in common than you might think." Deena produced some cheese and crackers from her blue nautical tote bag and laid them out on a small tray, which she passed around.

"How so?" Cole took a cracker and glanced at Sam.

"Well, you're both hard workers," Deena said.

"And you both chose a profession where you can help others," Chuck added.

Sam's eyes narrowed. She still had no idea what Cole did. "You help others?"

Cole nodded. "Sort of. Not as much as you. I'm in law enforcement."

"Oh." That was not what Sam had been expecting, given her previous suspicions of him being a con man. But someone in law enforcement would hardly be running scams on widows—further proof that she'd been wrong about Chuck and Cole.

Deena nibbled a little bit of cheese. "Sam, you help

people at the worst time of their lives, when their relationships are falling apart and they've been betrayed by the person they thought was closest to them. You help them get what they deserve out of the divorce. You help them get justice." Deena turned to Cole. "And Cole, you help people get justice as well at an even worse time of their lives, when someone has been killed or kidnapped or a heinous crime has been committed."

Sam looked at Cole with new eyes. "I guess we kinda do have that in common."

"I guess so." Cole smiled at her, the setting sun highlighting the flecks of amber in his green eyes, and for the first time, she thought she saw a look of warmth in their depths. Maybe they could be friends after all.

That made the task of returning Chuck's wallet to Saltwater Sweets all the more important.

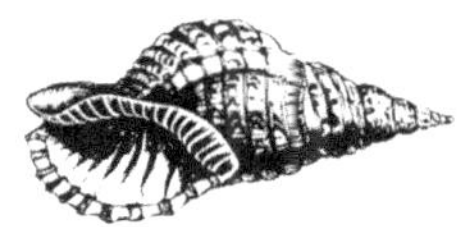

CHAPTER 18

Gina was having a hard time believing the story Hugh was spinning.

They'd moved into her space in the storage room because Hugh claimed that his life was in danger if certain people found out where he was. Gina hadn't envisioned finding Hugh this way. She should probably turn him in to the police, but this could be her only chance to get her money back. He probably wouldn't be able to pay her any money from inside a jail cell.

"I swear I had no idea Holly had taken the money." Hugh looked down at his feet, his cheeks turning red. "I thought we were just running off together."

Gina crossed her arms over her chest. She was over Hugh and didn't have feelings for him, but it still stung that he was so intent on running away with Holly that he didn't even notice she had been embezzling money. Then again, Hugh was an accomplished liar and would say almost anything to manipulate her, so he could have made that part up.

"Didn't you think it was weird that, all of a sudden, she had all this money?" Gina asked. "And what about our personal savings account? How would she get into that?"

"Well, that part actually was me. But I figured since I was leaving you with the entire business and all the business accounts, we were even." Hugh gave her that faux-innocent look that had always worked in the past.

Not this time.

"I see. So you were just going to take all of our money, disappear, and live on some tropical island happily ever after with Holly?"

"I don't know what I was thinking. I lost my mind. But as soon as I found out what she'd done to the business, I got the heck out of there."

Trying to save his own hide, as usual.

"So let me get this straight. You left all the money with Holly and came back here… for what?"

"I didn't leave *all* the money. Our savings was in a separate account from what Holly had taken. I managed to salvage that and maybe a little more. But the problem is now the authorities think I took all that money, and even worse, so does Mark Richards, the big developer who had put all that money down on his office renovation."

Gina wouldn't be surprised if Hugh was lying and trying to blame it all on Holly because he was now clearly in some sort of trouble. It didn't matter. What *did* matter was Hugh had their money, and that meant she had a chance to get her half back.

"Actually, I'm more afraid of Richards than of the police." Hugh gave a nervous laugh. "That's why I've been looking for you. You're the only one who can help me."

"Wait. You've been *looking* for me?" Was Hugh the person Ellie had heard about? Gina hoped so because anyone else looking for her would be a lot scarier.

"Yes. I didn't realize you changed your last name. We're not even divorced." Somehow, Hugh managed to sound like he was the one who had been wronged.

"It's pretty hard to divorce someone when you can't find them," Gina said. "I didn't want to be associated with you anymore, so I changed my name legally. How did you know I was in Shell Cove?"

"I did some digging. Contacted someone who we used to know and would help me. They mentioned something about a seaside motel, and I remembered your grandmother had owned this one."

Gina stared at him. She didn't even want to know who it was that had mentioned Shell Cove. Clearly, Hugh had some resources if he'd done some "digging" that resulted in Ellie finding out someone was looking for her. But what exactly did he want with her? Hopefully, he wasn't entertaining thoughts of them getting back together.

"What do you want?"

Hugh took a deep breath. "I need your help. You're the only one who can save me."

"My help? Why would I help you after what you did to me?"

He tried the puppy dog look. She was immune to that now. She didn't want to help him either. She wanted him to go to jail, but not before she got her share of the money.

"For old times' sake?" Hugh ventured.

Gina shook her head. "Not for old times' sake. For my half of our life savings. You owe me that at least."

Hugh shuffled his feet as if he was going to argue. "Well, I don't know."

"Okay, fine. No help. I'll just call the police, then." Gina grabbed her phone.

"No, no!" Hugh held his hand up. "Half the money. I suppose that's only fair. But only if you have what I need."

Was he referring to the document she'd taken?

"What's that?" She asked, just in case he was referring to something else. She didn't want to tip her hand.

"I think you might have a document. It was in the safe in my home office. I never got a chance to go back in for it because Holly and I had to leave so abruptly." Hugh looked at her hopefully. "You did know about the safe, right?"

"Yeah, I knew about the safe. And figured out your combination."

"So you have the document?" Hugh's relief was evident in the tone of his voice and set of his shoulders. He must really have been in trouble.

"Yes, I have it. What is it?"

Hugh let out a sigh and collapsed into the over-stuffed chair. "It's the thing that can keep me from getting killed. Mark Richards doesn't take lightly to being crossed, and he tends to settle his issues with base-ball bats and guns. Holly was so stupid to take that money. And honestly, Gina, I thought we would leave you with the thriving business, so I felt like taking our savings was a fair trade. That document has some dirt on Mark Richards that I can use to get him to back off, and it might even keep me from having too long of a jail sentence."

Gina didn't really have any options. She had to believe Hugh. It didn't really matter as long as she got her money. Then she could be rid of him, and who cared what happened to him after that? She wasn't the meek little lamb that he'd married, though. She was going to make sure she got her money first.

"Can you get the money into my bank account?"

Hugh nodded. "If I can get on the internet, I can transfer it." He glanced around the room. "So where's the document?"

"Not so fast. Money transfer first."

Hugh's eyes narrowed. "At least let me see it. Then I'll transfer." She thought she saw a new respect for her in his eyes.

"I wasn't stupid enough to keep it here at the motel. It's in my safety deposit box at the bank."

"Great! You go get it first thing tomorrow, and when you come back, I'll wire the money into your account."

"Well, that might be a little bit of a problem. The bank is closed until Tuesday for the town celebration."

"Tuesday? But that's two days away." Hugh settled back in his chair. "I guess I'll have to hide out there until then."

Gina did not relish the idea of having Hugh underfoot until then, but what else could she do? She couldn't let him live outside. Ironically, she needed to make sure he stayed safe until she got her money.

Hugh was looking around the room as if sizing it up for his stay. She'd fixed it up with furniture she'd found in storage, but it was still sort of small, especially for the two of them. And there was only one bed.

"You can stay on the couch." She pointed at the small love seat she'd put in the corner.

"Okay. This town is kind of nice. And the motel is quaint. It's not the high-powered real estate life you're used to, but you seem to have settled in." His gaze met hers. "You've changed, and it suits you. Oh, and by the way, I love your pies. When did you learn to make those?"

"You've tasted my pies?"

"Yeah. If you don't want someone nibbling the crust, maybe you shouldn't leave them in the windowsill. Sorry if I ruined the pie, but I was starving."

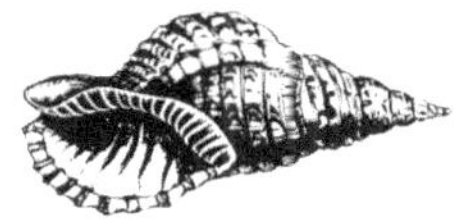

CHAPTER 19

Cole lingered in the Beachcomber motel parking lot with Sam. They'd driven their separate cars home from the marina where his dad kept the sailboat and had arrived at the same time. Now, they were standing a safe distance of four feet from each other halfway in between their rooms.

Cole was surprised at how much he'd enjoyed her company that day and how reluctant he was to say good night. It was dark now, and the sound of the waves, the stars twinkling in the sky, and the slight floral scent in the air made it feel like they were at the tail end of a date, the part of the date where he would typically kiss the girl. But this was no date, and kissing Sam would probably be something he regretted later on.

"Today was really fun. I haven't seen my mom this happy in a while." Sam's eyes twinkled in the moonlight, and Cole resisted the urge to step closer.

"My dad seems happy too. I never pictured him to

be the type to make chocolates." Cole shrugged. "I guess if he likes doing it…"

Sam laughed, and Cole took a step backward. Yep, he could definitely get caught up in that laugh. Best to put some distance between them. A noise over at the motel caught his attention, and he glanced over. All the windows were dark, which was unusual. Didn't Gina usually leave a light on?

Sam followed his gaze. "The motel looks kind of weird. Maybe Gina lingered downtown after the celebration?"

That must have been it, except there was that weird noise again.

"Do you hear voices from over there?" Cole asked.

They were silent for a few beats, both straining to listen, but there were no voices.

"I thought I heard something. Maybe just the waves." Sam yawned.

"Well, I guess we should get some sleep." Cole started toward his door.

"I'm beat. Sailing takes a lot out of you." Sam paused at her door and looked over at him. "Good night."

"Night."

Cole brushed his teeth, wondering if Sam was brushing hers at the same time on the other side of the wall. What did she wear to bed? Did she sleep on her side or her back? Cole pushed those thoughts from his mind and got into bed.

As he drifted off, he felt content, happy even. He hadn't felt that way in a long time.

He hadn't seen his father this happy since before his mom got sick. Apparently, all his worry had been for nothing. He had been overreacting about Deena, just like Audrey had suggested.

He turned on his side and looked out through the gap in the curtains, toward the motel lobby. Maybe he wasn't overreacting about his suspicions that something odd was going on at the motel.

Sam turned down the bedsheets and fluffed her pillow. It felt strange that Cole was just on the other side of the wall, probably going through a similar bedtime routine. She'd been surprised at how much she'd enjoyed his company at the town celebration and also later when they'd gone sailing.

And tonight, when they'd lingered outside their motel room doors, she thought that maybe he… well, it didn't matter what she'd thought. They seemed to be getting along, and that was good, especially since it appeared that their parents planned to be together for a long time.

She had to admit that Chuck really did seem to care for her mother. She hadn't seen any evidence that he was trying to take over the business, either, which made the fact that she still had his wallet tucked away among the underwear in her drawer weigh heavily. She had to return that as soon as possible.

So what if she'd feel guilty for years? Confessing to her mother and Chuck about it would serve no useful purpose. Better to slip it between the desk and wall and let them think it had fallen down in there.

Good thing she didn't hire the investigator that worked for her law firm to dig into Chuck in that system that used the Social Security numbers. That would've been a huge invasion of privacy. It was embarrassing that she was even considering going that far. What had she been thinking?

She glanced over at her laptop. She had several windows open to articles she'd dug up last night while researching Chuck's name on the internet. She hadn't had a chance to look through all of them yet. And she wasn't going to, either.

She closed the laptop and shoved it into the laptop bag.

There. Now she could go to sleep with a clear conscience. Well, almost clear. She still had the wallet to deal with. All she had to do was get to Saltwater Sweets before her mother or Chuck and stuff it between the desk and the wall and pretend like she'd never been there. Easy peasy.

CHAPTER 20

*S*am knew her mother always got in to Saltwater Sweets at 7:00 a.m., and she imagined Chuck didn't come any earlier, so she headed over at six.

She parked on the street two shops down and then hurried into the alley to let herself in the back door. At this time of morning, no one was open except for Ocean Brew, which already had a steady flow of customers. Thankfully, no one noticed her.

It felt strange sneaking around inside her own family store, but it was the only solution, and the quicker she got in and out, the better.

She hurried to the office and crawled under the desk to wedge the wallet up between the side of the desk and the wall. There was a little lip on the metal frame of the desk, and she balanced the wallet on the edge of that.

Her mother and Chuck had likely already looked all around the desk, but hopefully, they hadn't pulled it out from the wall, or if they had, she would convince them that it hadn't fallen down because it was caught on the lip.

All she needed to do now was "help" them find it.

She locked the door and skulked back out to the street, peeking out from the alleyway like some sort of foreign spy to make sure no one was watching. No one was, so she darted out and walked along to her car as if she'd simply been walking along the Main Street.

She was just opening the driver's side door when she heard…

"Sam! What are you doing here?"

Her heart crashed as she turned toward the familiar voice coming from the other side of the street: Cole.

What in the world was Sam doing here at six thirty in the morning? Cole had assumed she'd be getting ready to do yoga on the beach. Which was kind of why *he* was here. He'd planned on picking up some coffees and *accidentally* running into her on the beach.

His gaze flicked down the street toward Saltwater Sweets. Had she come from there? But her car was parked two shops down. Why wouldn't she park right in front or in the small lot in back?

"Hi!" Sam waved from the other side of the street, her smile bright as she crossed toward him. "I was just coming to Ocean Brew." She leaned toward him and lowered her voice. "The coffee at the Beachcomber leaves a bit to be desired. What are you doing here?"

Cole turned toward the coffee shop. She was coming here? Weird, because it looked like she'd been getting *into* her car, not *out* of it. Though he couldn't say he blamed her, the stuff at the motel was pretty awful, and he'd made a few trips here himself since he'd come to town.

"Same. Since we're both here, let's grab coffee together," he suggested.

"Great idea."

They went in and ordered their coffees. Sam didn't hesitate when he suggested they sit in the corner booth overlooking the street.

"Do you think our parents have recovered from the sailing trip?" Cole joked.

Sam laughed. "I don't know. I think that was a big day for them. I'm barely recovered myself."

"Me too. It was a good day, though," Cole ventured.

Sam nodded. "It was."

Cole let his gaze drift out over the main street of Shell Cove. It was a nice street, much different from the cities and sleazy back alleys he was used to. It was quaint and clean and happy.

"You know, I never realized how much I missed doing things like sailing… or just getting away from work and having fun."

Sam seemed to consider that. "Me either. I've spent the last few years building up my clientele, and that's involved just more and more work. I hardly even noticed it happening, but it seems like all I do now is work."

"I can relate to that. What you're doing is important. It helps people."

She smiled. "Sort of, but maybe I'm getting a little burned out. This week, working in the chocolate shop gave me a different perspective. Maybe I need to make a change in my life."

Their eyes met, and Cole said, "This week has given me a different perspective too."

Cole sipped his coffee, for the first time considering if maybe he needed to make a change in his life too.

Chuck did a double take as he passed Ocean Brew. Was that Cole and Sam sitting in the corner booth by the window?

They looked awfully cozy, chatting over coffee and laughing. He smiled to himself. Things were working out exactly as he'd hoped.

Now, he could move forward with his plans for Deena. He took the business card out of his pocket: Ashford Jewelers. He'd been there last week, looking at engagement rings.

In some ways, it felt like it was too soon, but he knew Deena was the one he wanted to spend the rest of his life with, and at their age, why wait? Especially now that Sam and Cole seemed to be coming around. He knew his daughter Audrey approved of the relationship already, so now there would be no objections.

Of course, he still didn't know if Deena would say yes, but he sure hoped so.

He unlocked the door to Saltwater Sweets and went inside.

Walking past the office on his way to the front, he glanced in, bending down to look on the floor again. He'd already done this several times as well as searching the desk and even pulling it out from the wall, but there was no sign of his wallet. It wasn't at his apartment either.

Maybe he'd left it in the front room of the shop.

He pulled out his phone and called the jewelry store. Cradling the phone between his ear and shoulder, he unwrapped the fudge to put it in the front window. Penuche, rocky road, chocolate, peanut butter. He lined them up beside each other in delicious, creamy blocks.

"I'd like to put a deposit on that marquise engagement ring I looked at last week," he explained to the sales lady after telling her who he was.

"That's wonderful! I'm sure she'll be delighted."

"Well, I hope so, but don't forget it's a surprise, so remember… Deena must *not* find out about this."

Deena hummed under her breath as she let herself in through the back door of Saltwater Sweets. Yesterday had gone better than she'd hoped. She really felt like she had won Cole over, and Sam seemed to be warming to Chuck.

Chuck's car was parked in the little lot out back, and she couldn't wait to discuss it with him. He was probably putting the fudge out in the window display right now. They liked to change out what was on display every few days and had agreed to feature fudge for the rest of the week. If she hurried, she could help him with that and also rearrange the dark chocolates before her hair appointment.

She was about to call out his name when she heard him talking in the front room.

She hesitated for second.

"... Deena must *not* find out about this."

Her heart jolted. What in the world was he talking about? Who was he talking to, and what could she not find out about?

Now she was flustered, her mind whirling as she felt her world crashing. Part of her wanted to turn and flee out the door. But she wouldn't do that. Maybe she had misheard or was making too big of a deal out of it. Even if she wasn't making too big a deal out of it, she certainly wasn't going to run out of her own shop. Thoughts of all the things Sam had been subtly trying to warn her about bubbled up. What if Sam had been right all along? She was a lot savvier in these things than Deena.

Some inner instinct told her she shouldn't let on about what she had overheard. It could be totally innocent. It was never smart to jump to conclusions, and she needed some time to think.

She took a deep breath to compose herself and plastered a smile on her face then continued to the front room. "Good morning. You're in early."

Chuck turned around, slightly startled. Was that a look of guilt on his face? But then he smiled that warm smile that lifted her heart.

"Yes, dear. I thought I'd come in and put the fudge in the window. And now that we have a few minutes alone…" Chuck opened his arms for a hug, and Deena had no choice but to walk into them.

She tried not to stiffen as she returned the hug.

CHAPTER 21

Chuck gave Deena a peck on the cheek. Was she acting a little bit odd? It was probably his guilty conscience. He wasn't good at keeping things from people, but he really wanted the ring to be a surprise.

"Are you feeling okay?" Chuck asked.

Deena smiled. "Oh, I'm fine. Just my stomach is a little upset."

"You did eat a lot at the picnic yesterday," Chuck joked, and Deena laughed.

Her laugh sounded normal, so things must be okay.

They worked together arranging the fudge in the window. Chuck saw Sam and Cole coming out of the coffee house.

"I saw Sam and Cole having coffee together in Ocean Brew this morning," he said.

"Really?" Deena looked surprised. "Seems like they must be getting along, then."

"Yes, in fact, they looked quite chummy." Chuck waved to them from the window as they approached the door.

"Morning!" Sam breezed into the room with Cole following her.

"Smells great in here," Cole said.

"Always does." Sam grabbed one of her favorite chocolate turtles and bit in then turned to Chuck. "I was thinking maybe you could show me around the new website."

"I'd be delighted." Chuck was pleasantly surprised.

Sam seemed eager to have him show her what he had done. Her previous air of suspicion had vanished. Things really were looking up.

Sam picked another turtle out of the case, and they went into the back room. Chuck logged in and swiveled the monitor slightly so everyone could see. He showed them the site navigation and some of the back-end administrative screens.

"That's really great. So much better than what we had before." Sam went to take a bite of her chocolate but fumbled it, and it fell on the floor.

"Oh darn!" Sam looked down regretfully.

"I'll get it." Cole started to bend down, but Sam waved him off. "No. No, I'll get it. It rolled way under."

Sam dropped onto all fours, and Chuck pushed his chair back as she rooted around under the desk.

"Got it! Oh wait, what's this?" Sam backed out, holding a dusty chocolate and something else, Chuck's wallet.

"That's my wallet. But what was it doing under there? We looked under there pretty good." Chuck glanced at Deena, who shrugged.

"I think it got wedged between the desk and the wall. I saw part of it hanging down." Sam handed it to him.

Chuck dusted it off and peered inside. Everything seemed to be there. "That's weird. We looked down in there."

"There's a little lip on the side. See over here." Sam pointed at the little lip on the other side of the desk. "I guess it must have gotten stuck on that."

Chuck frowned. He supposed it was possible, but… suddenly, he was getting an uneasy feeling, and judging by the look on Cole's face, he was getting one too.

It was a struggle for Sam to keep the guilt she felt from showing up on her face. She felt like a jerk, lying to everyone about the wallet. But it was too late to tell the truth now.

Was it her imagination, or was Cole looking at the wallet suspiciously? Chuck seemed a bit odd now too. Even her mother seemed out of sorts.

Her guilty conscience must be getting to her. Maybe yoga would help. Either way, she needed to get out of Saltwater Sweets.

"Thanks for showing me the website. I gotta run." Sam tried to keep her voice light and her movements casual as she grabbed her purse from the table beside the back door.

"I'll walk out with you." Deena patted her hair and glanced at Chuck. "I have a hair appointment, so I'll be gone for a while."

Chuck kissed her on the cheek. Did her mother not seem as receptive to that as usual? Probably just her imagination.

Out on the street, Deena walked Sam to her car. "It's nice that you and Cole are getting along now."

"Yeah, he's not so bad. Chuck seems to be a good guy too," Sam said.

Deena frowned. "Yes. Well, things aren't always as they seem. Oh, I better run. Almost late for my appointment."

As Sam drove to the Beachcomber, her stomach grumbled. Apparently, those chocolate turtles hadn't done the trick. She'd seen Gina getting a tray of coffees and a bag of muffins at Ocean Brew. Maybe she was putting out a continental breakfast at the hotel.

She parked in front of her room and then headed over to the lobby, but it was empty. There were no muffins set out, only the ancient Mr. Coffee bubbling away on the counter.

Gina came out of the storeroom. "Oh. Sam. I didn't know anyone was in here." She glanced behind her nervously.

"I thought you might be having a continental break-fast in here," Sam said. "I'm starving."

"Breakfast? Nope. No breakfast. If you're hungry, I

have pie in the kitchen, though." Gina hurried over toward the kitchen as if she couldn't get away from the storeroom quickly enough.

"I think I'll pass on the pie. I just ate some candy and don't want to get too much of a sugar high, but thanks."

Sam headed toward the door, feeling as if Gina was watching her. It was almost as if Gina didn't want her nosing around the motel lobby, almost as if she were hiding something.

CHAPTER 22

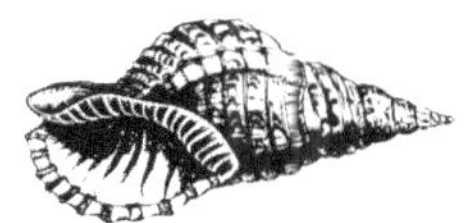

"I'm really glad to have my wallet back." Chuck smoothed his fingers over the familiar worn leather and then slipped it into his pocket. "It's not just my license or the credit cards. This wallet is sentimental because you gave it to me."

Cole's heart warmed at his father's words, but it was overshadowed by his suspicions about the missing wallet suddenly turning up. "Yeah, it's weird, though, that it was in the office the whole time."

Chuck's expression darkened. "I guess. Maybe I didn't look as well for it as I thought."

"I'm glad you have it now."

Cole hoped his father didn't pick up on the tone of suspicion in his voice. It was weird how Sam had suddenly dropped the candy on the floor and come up with the wallet. And Deena had been acting strange too. Maybe his initial suspicions of them had been right after all.

He hoped not. He was getting used to the idea of Sam not being the enemy—maybe even being a friend… or more.

He flashed back to when he'd seen her at her car earlier this morning. He could have sworn she was getting into the car and changed direction when he called out to her. But what would she have been doing here if she wasn't coming to Ocean Brew? Had she been in Saltwater Sweets? But if so, why not say so?

Should he mention it to his father? He already looked like something was on his mind.

While Cole was mulling over whether or not to tell Chuck, the door opened, and the three senior citizens he'd met at the town celebration came bustling in.

"Hello there," Rose said. "Did you all enjoy yourselves at the town celebration?"

"Of course," Chuck said.

Cole nodded. "I did. You have a nice little town here."

"Where is Deena?" Pearl asked, craning her neck to look in the back.

"She went to get her hair done," Chuck said.

"Oh, I see. I'd like some nonpareils. I know you can box them up as well as Deena can," Pearl said.

While Chuck was scooping out the candies, the door opened, and a woman with dark hair came in. Cole recognized her as the woman he'd seen on the back porch of the Beachcomber, talking to Sam and Gina.

"Ellie! How are you doing, dear?" Rose asked the woman.

"Good, and you?" Ellie hugged Rose and Pearl then turned to Leena. "Hi, Mom."

"Hi, El. Have you met Chuck's son, Cole?" Leena gestured to Cole.

Ellie looked at him with a flicker of recognition. "I think we met briefly at the motel."

Leena beamed at her daughter. "She never forgets a face. That's why she's such a great private investigator."

Ellie laughed. "Well, there might be other reasons, but thanks."

Cole smiled, but inwardly his mind was racing. Private investigator? Why had Sam been talking to a private investigator?

Suddenly, he realized that the friendly vibes he'd gotten from Sam had all been a lie. The whole time, she was having his father investigated, most likely to find out how much money he had and how they could best work an angle to get it. Meanwhile, she'd been acting friendly, trying to lull them into a false sense of security, and it had almost worked. Almost, but not quite.

CHAPTER 23

Sam shoved her rolled-up yoga mat into the closet and flopped down on the bed. Contrary to what she'd thought, yoga hadn't helped soothe her guilty conscience.

But it wasn't just guilt over the wallet that was bothering her. She'd sensed something was off with Chuck and Cole. And what had her mother meant when she'd said things weren't always as they seemed?

Just this morning, things had seemed so bright, but now… she wasn't sure what to think.

She'd planned on leaving town in a few days, but maybe she should think about staying on until next week. That reminded her she needed to check her emails to see if there were any emergencies at the office.

She flipped up her laptop screen and logged into the computer. All the windows with the articles she'd found about Chuck on the internet appeared.

Maybe it wouldn't hurt if she scrolled through them just a little bit.

An article caught her eye: "Local Man Invests in Business, Makes a Bundle."

What was that about?

She quickly scanned the article. Apparently, Chuck had invested in a woman's dry cleaning business. Mary Newcomb. There was a picture of them standing side by side. He had his arm around her, and they both had big smiles on their faces. Had he been romantically involved with her too?

Apparently, her business had been struggling until Chuck invested in it. It didn't say if the two were romantically involved, but they sure looked chummy in the picture. What the article did say, however, was that Chuck had negotiated a stake in the business. The business took off, and he ended up profiting. Though the article didn't name specific numbers, it did say he'd made quite a big profit.

Did her mother know about this Mary Newcomb?

Thus far, Sam had had no evidence to back up her suspicions of Chuck, but this article changed things. Before she thought things through, she was on the phone to her mother.

"Hi, Mom. How did your hair come out?"

Deena sighed. "Oh, you know. The same." Sam sensed a note of dejection in her mother's voice.

"You don't like it? Maybe you need a hairstyle change."

"Maybe I need a lot of things to change," Deena said.

That was odd. Her mother hardly ever talked that way. Something was up.

"Maybe. Say, Mom, did Chuck ever mention a Mary Newcomb?"

There was hesitation on the other end then, "I don't think so, why?"

"Did he mention he owned a business with someone else?"

"No. Sam, what is this about?"

"I hope you won't be upset, but I just happened to do a little surfing on the internet, and an article about Chuck came up. Apparently, he was involved with this Mary Newcomb and owns part of her business." Sam paused, gnawing on her bottom lip. How far should she go with her suspicions? There was a chance that this could all be innocently explained. Her mother might never forgive her if she accused Chuck of something and was wrong. Heck, she might not forgive herself.

"He never mentioned it, but to be fair, I haven't told him exactly everything about myself, either. He did say I was the first woman he was involved with since his wife died, though. Are you sure he was involved with this other woman?"

"Well, I guess I'm not exactly sure. They could be just friends. But did he ever mention anything about taking over part ownership of Saltwater Sweets or acquiring an equity stake in it?"

"No. He did offer to put up the money to invest in

one of those new, expensive candy-making machines. Our equipment is so old, and I don't really have any money," Deena said. "He never said anything about owning part of the business, but I did overhear him say something odd this morning."

"What?"

"Honestly, I've been in a tizzy about it all day. He was in the front room, talking on the phone, and I heard him say, 'Deena must not find out about this.'"

"Find out about what?" Sam asked.

"That's the thing. I have no idea. And I was too frazzled to confront him. In fact, I've been avoiding him ever since."

She knew it. Chuck really had been up to no good, which meant that Cole was also up to no good. Well, if they thought they were going to put one over on Sam and her mother, they had another think coming.

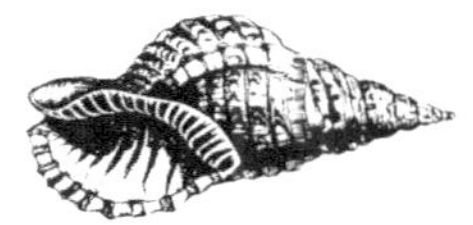

CHAPTER 24

*C*ole waited for the welcome-wagon ladies to leave then turned to Chuck.

"I saw Sam talking to that private investigator before."

Chuck frowned. "So? Sam grew up here. They're probably friends."

"I don't know. She was at the motel, and they were out on the back porch, and when I approached, they stopped talking as if they didn't want me to hear what they were saying." Cole glanced out the window to make sure that Deena wasn't on her way back. "What if she's having you investigated?"

A cloud of uncertainty settled on him. What if Sam and Ellie really *were* just friends and the conversation had been innocent? Maybe they'd been gossiping or talking "girl talk," and that's why they stopped talking. He didn't want to mess things up for his father, but he also didn't want him to get taken advantage of, and he had to admit Sam and Deena had been acting very strange this morning.

However, when he'd had coffee with Sam, she'd been fine. Except when he'd first seen her at her car, she'd seemed a little nervous. And hadn't he thought she was opening the car door and not closing it?

"I think you're making something out of nothing," Chuck said, though Cole could tell his father was thinking about it. Had his dad picked up on the strange vibe from Deena and Sam too?

"It's not like Sam and Ellie would be good friends. There's a big age difference between them. And the way they were talking on the porch… well…" Cole glanced down the hallway. "And what was up with that wallet business? Do you think it really could've gotten lodged beside the desk? It seems weird that Sam dropped her chocolate and came up with the wallet, doesn't it?"

And why had Sam taken off right after she'd found it?

Chuck pressed his lips together. "Well, now that you mention it, that was rather odd. Deena was acting kind of strange when she came in this morning. Not her usual, affectionate self."

"As if she knew something weird might be about to happen?" Cole asked.

"Maybe. But I don't think so. I know her. She's a good person."

"Dad, plenty of good people do bad things. In my line of work, I've seen people who seem like the nicest people in the world end up being the biggest dirtbags. Now, I'm not saying Deena is up to something, but maybe we should be cautious."

Cole glanced around the store. His father had made improvements to the store and the website. He'd been learning the business. "Has she asked you to invest into the business... you know... buy new shelves or software?"

"I can't say as she asked outright, but she did mention something about a new chocolate tempering machine that is very expensive. She can't afford it, and well..." He looked at Cole sheepishly. "I did kind of volunteer to buy it."

Had he volunteered, or had she cleverly manipulated him into "volunteering"? Cole didn't want to say that out loud and make his father feel worse.

"You know what? I think I might need to take the afternoon off." Chuck pulled his phone out of his pocket. "I'm going to message Deena and let her know that I won't be here after lunch."

CHAPTER 25

It was late afternoon by the time Gina got back to the storage room with sandwiches for Hugh. She couldn't wait for the bank to open so she could get rid of him. This was all feeling a little too familiar, and she didn't like waiting on him one bit.

"Tuna is my favorite." Hugh beamed up at her. "You remembered."

"They were the first sandwiches I came to in the grocery store." Gina certainly hadn't gotten his favorite on purpose. She didn't want to do anything to encourage him as he'd been hinting there might be a future for them. There wouldn't be, but she was hesitant to come right out and say it, lest her rejection make him think twice about transferring the money.

She was surprised to discover that she really was over Hugh and, even though he did look rather pathetic, she could muster only the smallest amount of sympathy for him.

"Look, you just need to stay in here and be quiet for one more day. Tomorrow, the bank will be open, and I can get that document. I'll take pictures of it with my phone so you can verify that I have it, but I'm not handing it over until you transfer the money." She wasn't the naïve, trusting person she'd been when they were married.

"Okay. I guess that's fair." Hugh tucked into his sandwich.

"And then what do you plan to do once you have it?"

"I'm not sure. Maybe contact the authorities?"

That didn't sound like a well-thought-out plan, and Gina was afraid that Hugh might be up to something. She didn't really care about that, but what if whatever he had planned got her involved in this mess somehow? She didn't trust Mark Richardson and had to make sure Hugh handed over that document to the police so Mark would be out of the picture.

Should she take Ellie into her confidence about Hugh being at the motel and get her advice? Before she could think that through, Jules's voice rang out from the lobby.

"Gina, where are you?"

"Hey, is that your cousin Jules?" Hugh asked.

Gina rushed to the door, turning and hissing at Hugh, "Quiet. Don't make a sound."

Gina slipped out into the lobby. "Jules! So great to see you. What are you doing here?"

Jules looked confused. "I'm here to help run the motel. It's what I do."

"Right. I know. But it's slow. I'm handling things fine. Why don't you go off with Nick? Isn't the bank closed today? He must have the day off."

Gina kept the smile on her as she stood in between Jules and the storage room. Maybe she'd overdone it because Jules frowned and glanced over her shoulder toward the door. "Were you talking to someone in there?"

"Talking? No. Talking to myself. Bad habit."

How in the world was she going to get rid of Jules? Her cousin didn't look like she was going to budge.

"Would you like some pie? I baked fresh apple."

"No, I don't need any pie. Why don't you take off? Do some shopping or something." Jules was definitely here to stay.

Maybe Gina could come up with some task that would get her out of the lobby. Cleaning the rooms, perhaps, or—

Whoosh!

But just then, the unmistakable sound of the toilet flushing rang through the lobby. Stupid Hugh! Didn't he realize they could hear that?

Jules's frown deepened.

"Was that the toilet? But I thought we were alone…" Jules's expression took on a smirk. "Oh. Now I see why you were trying to get rid of me. You have a guy here."

Gina made a face. As if. "No, I don't… oh yes, yes. And I'd like some privacy."

"Who is it? Are you hiding him in the storeroom? Is it that cute guy, Dean, from the restaurant? Or is it that landscaper, Kyle?" To Gina's horror, Jules headed toward the kitchen.

The bathroom that Gina used was in the hallway between the kitchen and the back door to the storeroom. Hugh must have used the back door that led to that hall. Gina ran after Jules but couldn't stop her. The bathroom door opened, and Hugh stepped out.

The look of disbelief on Jules's face was almost comical. "Hugh? Your secret boyfriend is your ex-husband?"

"You expect me to believe you had nothing to do with embezzling from the company?" Jules glanced from Hugh to Gina.

They were back in the storage room, filling Jules in on how Hugh had come to be hiding out there. Jules had been surprised to learn about the embezzling and that Gina and Hugh hadn't had an amicable divorce, but she didn't make a big deal out of it, much to Gina's relief.

"It's the truth." Hugh sounded offended that Jules didn't believe him.

"It doesn't really matter," Gina cut in. "That's

Hugh's problem to deal with. I just want my half of the money, and then he's on his own."

"And you need this document that's in the safety deposit box at the bank," Jules said.

Gina nodded. "I wasn't able to get there before the bank closed."

"I can call Nick and see if he'll open it early for us," Jules offered.

"No. Wait." Hugh looked between them nervously. "That might raise suspicion. And the fewer people that know the better."

Jules put her phone down. "Well then, what are you going to do? Just hang out here until tomorrow? And then what?"

"I guess I'll just find someplace else to go and figure out how to get myself out of this mess." Hugh looked so lonely and dejected that Gina almost felt sorry for him. Almost.

"It sounds like you don't have a good plan." Jules glanced at Gina.

"We were just talking about that when you came in," Gina said. "I know we don't want to involve any more people, but I was thinking that I already have Ellie searching for Hugh. She knows the situation and has contacts in law enforcement. She might be able to help you come up with a plan and figure out the right person to hand the document over to."

Hugh mulled this over then nodded slowly. "Okay. I guess we can tell her. But no one else."

Jules looked down at her phone and then nodded.

"Okay. I won't tell Nick. The bank opens tomorrow, so I guess it's not that long. But what are you going to do in the meantime?"

Gina shot Hugh a warning look. "In the meantime, he's going to hide out *quietly* in the storage room and hope no one else figures out he's here."

Cole poked a stick into the ashes where the fire on the beach had been. It was evident no one had been here the night before. Had the fugitive left town?

He walked a little farther down the beach but saw no sign of a fire, no footprints, no evidence of anyone being there.

He walked along the edge of the water on his way back to the Beachcomber. He removed his sandals and let the cold, foamy surf wash over the tops of his feet. Maybe the frigid water would give him clearer insight as to what was going on with Deena and Sam.

He knew he'd gotten his father thinking about Deena's intentions, but had he been right to mention things to his dad? He still had some doubts himself. Just because Ellie and Sam weren't the same age didn't mean that they weren't friends.

But that business with the wallet was definitely weird. And his dad had said Deena had been acting strange. The thing was that Cole had really been starting to like Sam and Deena. He didn't want to believe that they were up to something fishy. Then again, his father had mentioned engagement rings, and that was serious. Better for him to find out now before they get married.

As he walked up the steps from the beach, he saw Ellie rushing into the lobby of the motel. Was it his imagination, or was she glancing over her shoulder as if trying not to be seen?

Was Sam over there too? He scanned the lot, but Sam's car wasn't there. Maybe his imagination *was* getting the better of him. He should just go in his room and mind his own business. He'd already planted a seed of doubt in his father's mind, and he knew his dad was thinking things over. Now he needed to butt out and let his father come to the conclusion he found in his heart. And if he felt that Deena was pulling something shady, they could both get out of town as quickly as they wanted.

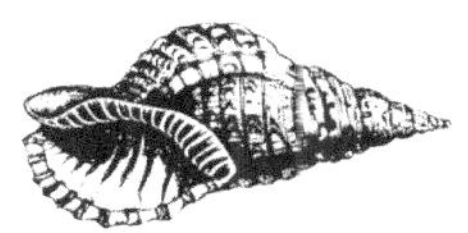

CHAPTER 26

It took a while for Gina to convince Ellie not to call the cops on Hugh. Ellie still seemed skeptical of Hugh's claim that he wasn't involved in the embezzling, but Gina didn't really care about that. All she wanted was the chance to give Hugh the document and get her money.

"Okay, I got a message back from my contact. The advice is to get the paperwork and have Hugh turn himself in. Things will go better for him if he does that voluntarily. And there happens to be an FBI contact right in town. My friend will hook us up."

"What do you think will happen to me?" Hugh asked.

Ellie shrugged. "Hopefully jail time."

"Jail time? But I didn't do anything." Hugh pouted.

"So you say," Ellie said. Then she added, "I did find out that Holly has been on the FBI's radar. Apparently, she's done this before. So you actually might have a shot at convincing them that you weren't involved in the embezzling."

"And what about the developer, Mark Richardson? He was into something really shady. I have it all down on that paper in the safety deposit box."

"If what you say is true, he'll get jail time."

"I guess that works. I'm more afraid of him than the FBI." Hugh settled back in his chair. He did look a bit relieved. Gina wasn't sure if she was glad or not.

"If you help turn this other guy in, you might get a lighter sentence." Ellie walked over and stood directly in front of Hugh, glaring down at him. "But you better not mess up the money transfer for Gina, or I'll make sure you regret it. I have friends that take a dim view of husbands not paying what they owe their wives, so you better think carefully about how you proceed after Gina shows you that document."

Sam sipped her cinnamon latte as she pulled into the Beachcomber Motel lot. She usually didn't drink coffee at night like this, but she had a feeling she might be up late tonight.

Her mother had been upset with the information she'd revealed about Chuck. She knew Deena needed time to think about it, but she figured her mom would eventually confront Chuck. But her mother was such a pushover. If Chuck begged her not to dump him, Sam thought she might need some moral support to keep her resolve.

A little part of Sam worried that she might be over-reacting. She knew from her clients' court cases that what she had was circumstantial. The article about Chuck and Mary Newcomb really didn't prove Chuck had done anything wrong. They had never asked him for an explanation, and he might have a reasonable one.

If only she could get some solid proof.

She recognized Ellie's car as she pulled into the parking lot. Should she hire Ellie to dig up that proof? She needed someone who could do it quickly, someone whom her mother would trust.

Instead of going to her room, she went over to the motel.

The lobby was empty. No one was out on the porch. No one was in the kitchen. She heard voices coming from a closed door on the side of the lobby.

She went over to the door. What was this room, anyway? Should she knock or just go in?

She's felt funny just going in, so she knocked. "Hello. It's Sam. Is anyone in there?"

The voices stopped. She heard shuffling and whispering, and then the door opened a crack, and Gina peered out. "Hi, Sam. I was just getting some stuff here in the storage room."

Sam could see Ellie standing behind Gina. "Oh, okay. I just came over to talk to Ellie." Sam peeked in farther to wave at Ellie, surprised to see that she wasn't the only one in there.

Jules was in there and a strange man Sam had never met. He looked a little scruffy, and the four of them were awfully crowded in that small room.

Suddenly unsure of what she'd stumbled onto, Sam looked from Gina to the others. "What's going on in here? Did I interrupt something?"

CHAPTER 27

Cole had been sitting in his room at the Beachcomber when movement out in the parking lot caught his eye.

Sam was back, but she wasn't going into her room. Instead, she was heading right for the lobby of the motel. Was she going to meet Ellie there?

Maybe they were working out another scheme for Deena to keep her claws in his father. Well, if Sam could sneak around, then so could he. And it just so happened he was very good at sneaking around.

He quietly slipped out of his door and pretended like he was walking toward the beach then veered off when he reached the corner of the main motel building. He skirted tight against the wall, stopping just shy of a window. He stopped and cocked his ear to listen but didn't hear anything. He peeked in. The lobby was empty.

Maybe they were in the kitchen.

He skulked along the side toward the kitchen window, ducking down and peering up over the sill. No one was there, either.

He checked the porch. Empty.

He went around the other side, peeking into a window that was a few feet down from the kitchen window. It looked like it went to a hallway. There was a door halfway down, and…wait a minute! Who was that guy?

He looked all scruffy and unshaven and a little bit familiar.

Cole pulled his phone out and scrolled to the picture that Gary had sent of the fugitive. It was him!

The fugitive was in the Beachcomber Motel. The fugitive was an embezzler. Was he working with Sam and Deena?

Now it all made sense. That's why the fugitive was here in this tiny seaside town. They were working on some kind of scam, likely to do with his father. Was Sam involved in some kind of embezzling or money-laundering ring? Is that what she and Deena were going to use his father for? To take his money or maybe use him as some sort of a fall guy?

His phone pinged as he was shoving it back in his pocket, but he didn't have time to answer it. He had to act quickly if he wanted to catch the fugitive and save his father from whatever Sam and Deena were up to.

He rushed back to his hotel room and grabbed his gun and his badge. Contrary to what he'd told Gary earlier, he actually had brought his badge. After years of carrying it everywhere, it had felt too strange to leave it home, so he'd put it in his luggage. After all, he was still part of the FBI. He wasn't fired or on leave, just an extended vacation. Looked like that had been a smart decision.

He rushed back over to the motel, certain he was doing the right thing. There was no way he was going to let anyone take advantage of his father and possibly put him in a position where he ran afoul of the law. Now, he could kill two birds with one stone. He could save his father and capture that fugitive that the FBI was looking for.

Gina didn't see as they had much choice but to explain everything to Sam. She'd already seen Hugh, and they didn't want her running around town, talking about some scruffy guy holed up at the motel. They needed to explain the situation so she would keep quiet.

"I've seen so many similar stories in my line of work." Sam patted Gina's arm in sympathy and shot Hugh an angry glare. "I hate it when the husbands take advantage."

"Yeah, me too." Ellie glared at Hugh also.

"I think your plan is a good one. Too bad we couldn't get that document sooner and get rid of him," Sam said.

"Hey, what do you mean by 'get rid of him'?" Hugh asked.

"Well, you can't stay in the storeroom forever," Jules said. "The sooner you surrender to Ellie's contact, the better."

"And the sooner Gina gets her money, the sooner she can put you in the past," Sam said.

"So, what now? We just wait until the bank opens tomorrow?" Sam asked.

"I guess so—"

Crash!

Everyone spun toward the door, which had just been kicked open. Cole was standing there with a gun pointing into the room.

"No one move! You're under arrest for harboring a fugitive!"

CHAPTER 28

efore Sam was even finished processing the situation, Ellie jumped in between them and Cole. Her own gun was drawn, and her expression was one of anger and suspicion.

"What do you think you're doing?" she demanded.

"Apprehending fugitives." Cole flipped out his badge. "I'm with the FBI. What do you think *you're* doing?"

"I'm a private investigator, as you know. And I'm in contact with the FBI about this situation. Which makes me a little suspicious of you busting in here." They both still had guns drawn as Ellie regarded Cole. "And by the way, we aren't harboring a fugitive. Well, technically, maybe we are, but the FBI is apprised of the situation."

"I *am* the FBI!" Cole said.

"Then why don't you know what's going on?" Ellie demanded.

Cole's phone pinged, and he wrestled it out of his pocket.

As Sam watched Cole read the message on his phone, her brain caught up with the situation.

Cole was in town on an assignment from the FBI to find a fugitive? He'd never mentioned that to them. He'd been lying and sneaking around about that the whole time. Apparently, that ran in the family.

Cole cleared his throat. "I see. The office has just notified me of your involvement in the situation. You can put your gun away."

Cole holstered his gun, and Ellie did the same.

"So, wait… you busted in here on some kind of a misunderstanding without having the whole story?" Gina gestured toward Cole's phone.

She looked worried, and Sam couldn't blame her. If Cole took Hugh into custody right now, he might not be able to transfer the money to Gina.

Cole ignored the question and scanned the room. "What are you all doing in here? Are you all involved in this?"

"What are *you* doing in here?" Sam blurted out. "How did you know we were in the storage room? Were you spying on us?"

Cole turned his gaze on her. His green eyes, normally so friendly, were dark and cold. "Spying? I think that's your department. And what is your association with this fugitive, anyway? Are you working together?"

"What are you talking about? I don't even know him! I came over to talk to Ellie." Sam was indignant.

Cole glanced at Ellie, who nodded.

"I'm not sure I can believe you. You lied about being at Saltwater Sweets this morning. You took my father's wallet and snuck in to wedge it under the desk so you could make that ridiculous show of dropping your chocolate and finding it, didn't you?"

Hugh, Gina, and Jules, who had been swiveling their heads to follow the conversation, raised their brows at Sam.

Her cheeks burned with embarrassment. "Okay. That's true. I admit I was wrong. I didn't mean to take your father's wallet. It was sort of an accident."

"An accident?" Cole was incredulous.

"It was on the desk, and I just peeked inside. I only wanted to see his Social Security number. I wanted to do a little background check on him and make sure he wasn't trying to pull a scam on my mother. But she caught me, and I had to put the wallet in my purse, and then, well… sneaking into the store in the morning before anyone got there was the only way I could return it."

"You're investigating my father?" Cole asked.

Sam crossed her arms over her chest and looked at the others, who were following the conversation like a television soap opera. Sam half expected one of them to get up and make popcorn. "Yeah. And a good thing too. I know what he did to Mary Newcomb. Was he planning to do the same to my mother?"

"Did your private investigator dig up that information?" Cole glanced at Ellie.

"What? No. I didn't hire a private investigator. I don't have Ellie digging into anything yet. I googled."

"Ellie is digging into things for me." Gina pointed to Hugh.

Cole barely heard her as his attention was fixed on Sam. "So you're making a judgement about my father based on something you found on the internet? For your information, Mary Newcomb was our cleaning lady. She wanted to start her own business, and my father generously offered to help her out. He didn't even want a cut of her business, but Mary insisted. She said her pride wouldn't let her take handouts."

Sam's gaze narrowed. She didn't quite buy that story, but he sounded so sincere. Except something didn't sit right. How had he known they had Hugh in here?

"You came bursting in here like you knew we were all here with Hugh. How did you know that?" Sam asked.

Now it was Cole's turn to be embarrassed. "Well, I saw Ellie's car, and then I saw you come over. I guess I didn't actually know that he was here, but I figured you two were up to something and wanted to find out what it was. Looks like I was right since you just admitted that you were investigating my father. I saw Hugh through the window and had no choice but to try to apprehend him."

"So you *were* spying on me!" Sam said.

"Maybe. But for good reason. I need to protect my father, and it's clear that you and your mother were planning to use him for his money to buy new equipment for Saltwater Sweets."

"What are you talking about? We haven't taken any of his money. I actually discussed this with my mother earlier today. She said he offered to pay for some new equipment, but she didn't really want to take him up on it. If anyone is up to something, it's your father. My mom overheard him telling someone that Deena must not find out about some big secret earlier today. He's hiding something, and I want to know what it is."

"You're right. He is hiding something. An engagement ring. He wanted it to be a surprise. That's what she can't find out."

"Awww, that's so sweet," Jules said, eliciting a frown from Cole.

It was kind of sweet. If it was true. But why would Cole make that up? And now that she thought about it, the article she'd read about Mary Newcomb had cast Chuck in a good light. It had never said anything about him taking advantage, and in fact, it had sounded like she wouldn't have been able to finance the business without him.

Had she just interpreted things in a negative way? Chuck had been working hard at getting them all to get along since she'd come to town. And he'd even restored that sailboat at no cost to her mother. Her mother had mentioned how delighted she'd been when he'd suggested it and how he had done all the work and paid for all the supplies.

"So you mean he's not trying to steal the business?"

Cole scowled. "No. Why would he? My dad has plenty of money of his own, as I'm sure you know."

"Actually, I don't know. My mother never mentioned anything about whether he had money, and I haven't done that kind of digging into his finances."

"I think maybe you guys have been making the wrong assumptions for the right reasons. I get that you wanted to protect your parents. That makes sense. But I've seen Deena and Chuck together, and those two are smitten with each other," Gina said. "I think the two of them just simply fell in love."

"I agree, and they're perfect for each other too," Jules added.

"And now we might've ruined it by getting them to suspect each other." Sam glanced up at Cole.

She felt like the worst kind of heel. Her mom deserved happiness, and so did Chuck.

"You both made a mistake. Lying and sneaking around is never good," Ellie said. "But it seems like you're even with each other now. But the important thing is to come clean with Chuck and Deena. Set things right so they can be happy together."

Cole glanced at Sam. "Maybe it's not too late."

Sam jumped up. "You're right. We have to find our parents and set the record straight."

She headed for the door, turning to look at Cole. "Are you with me?"

"Yeah. I'd hate to have ruined things for my dad."

"So I guess you're not taking me into custody right away, then?" Hugh asked hopefully.

Cole stopped and glanced back, looking torn between leaving with Sam or arresting Hugh. Ellie waved him off. "Don't worry. I'm not letting him go anywhere. He has a promise to fulfill for Gina first thing in the morning. After that, he's all yours."

Cole nodded at Hugh. "I guess you're going to get a small reprieve. Don't worry, though. Ellie will keep you in line."

Sam had been worried that they'd ruined her mother's and Chuck's relationship for good, but it turned out nothing was further from the truth. They were sitting in Deena's living room after having both texted their parents. It turned out their parents were a lot smarter than they were and had already figured out that everything was just a misunderstanding.

"So you see, we each messaged each other and then discovered it was just a bunch of misunderstandings." Chuck grabbed Deena's hand. "I'm sorry I ever doubted you, dear."

"I'm sorry too." Deena beamed at Chuck.

And he looked at her with that look of total love. Sam should've known when she'd seen him look at her like that before that all her suspicions were about nothing.

"I'm sorry I started it all." Sam put her coffee cup down. "And I'm really sorry I took your wallet, Chuck.

That was totally stepping over the line, and I was a jerk. Can you guys forgive me?"

"Of course, dear," Deena said. "We understand that the two of you were just trying to protect us."

Sam glanced over at Cole, who looked tongue-tied and embarrassed. "I really was. At least I thought I was. But I should've known better. I should have butted out and let my dad handle his own business. And I'm sorry that I introduced doubt into your relationship." He glanced at Sam, and his heart flipped. "I'm sorry that I doubted you, too, Sam."

"And Chuck, for what it's worth, I really do like you. You obviously treat my mom like gold, and I'd be happy to have you as my stepdad." Sam felt a little teary-eyed at Chuck's grateful look.

"Me too, Deena," Cole said. "You've been so nice to me since I've been here, and I treated you rotten. I'm delighted you make my dad happy, and I'm happy that you're in our lives."

"Well, it's a good thing you both feel that way because…" Deena held up her left hand, where the diamond ring sparkled. "We're getting married."

Sam jumped to her feet. "Congratulations!"

Chuck gave Sam a hug. Then Sam hugged her mom, whispering, "I truly wish the best of happiness for the two of you."

Cole was on his feet, too, hugging his father. Then Chuck kissed Deena, and Deena kissed Sam. Sam kissed Chuck. Deena kissed Cole. Then Cole kissed Sam.

Wait a minute. How did that happen?

But Sam had to admit even though it was an awkward moment they all laughed off, the small peck of a kiss felt right. And when she pulled back and looked up at Cole, she thought for a split second he gave her the same look Chuck had given her mother.

"Well, I'm happy to see the two of you getting along," Deena said after witnessing the kiss. Sam's cheeks burned.

"Me too," Chuck said.

"There is one thing," Deena said.

"What's that?" Sam asked.

Deena held up her finger with the big sparkly ring. "Once we're married, the two of you are going to be brother and sister."

CHAPTER 30

The next morning, Sam awakened feeling better than she had in years. Her mom was happy, Chuck wasn't screwing her over, and she and Cole had mended things after all their lies and suspicions. She was grateful everyone had forgiven her for the wallet incident.

She glanced at Cole's room as she walked past for her morning beach yoga. She was half hoping he might be down there meditating, but then she remembered that he had the Hugh situation to deal with.

Gina had planned to get to the bank the minute it was open, so after yoga, Sam changed and hurried over to the motel to check in on the situation.

Gina, Jules, Ellie, Hugh, and Cole were all in the storage room.

"This does look like it could help your case, Hugh." Ellie handed a stack of papers, which Sam assumed were the papers that had been in the safety deposit box, to Cole.

Cole glanced over them, nodding. "And make a case for prosecution of Mark Richards. Okay. I'm going to contact the office for further instructions." He whipped out his phone and went into the other room to make the call.

"Now you need to come through with your promise to Gina." Ellie stood in front of Hugh, her hands on her hips.

Gina shoved the laptop at him. "I've written my bank wire-transfer number on this sticky note. Don't be a jerk."

"Don't worry. I make good on my promises." Hugh managed to look offended as he started typing into the computer.

Cole came back into the room. "Gary says to hold him here, and they're going to send a car."

"Can do," Ellie said.

"There. It's transferred." Hugh turned the computer toward Gina, who bent over and scrolled around.

Gina straightened. "It's good. Thanks."

It was getting crowded in the storage room, so Sam decided to make her exit. "I'm glad things worked out. I'll see you all later."

To her surprise, Cole followed her out.

"So all's well that ends well," Cole said.

"I guess so. With our parents and with Gina."

Cole glanced back at the motel. "Yeah. I'm glad I

could help with that. I wasn't exactly keeping it from anyone that I worked for the FBI, you know."

"Yeah, I know. There have been a lot of misunderstandings, but I hope we can be friends now." She looked over at him.

"More than that. Looks like we'll be family."

The words warmed Sam's heart.

"What are you going to do now? Are you getting ready to go home?" Cole asked.

Sam sighed. "That's a good question. I don't want to go back to my stressful job. Being here in Shell Cove has made me take stock of my priorities."

They stopped at the end of the lot and looked out over the ocean. "I know what you mean. I was at a crossroads in my job, and now that I've been here, I'm wondering if it isn't time for a change. My dad isn't getting any younger, and spending time with him this week has made me realize how little time I've spent with him the last few years because of my job."

"You mean you're think about staying here?" The idea that Cole might stay in town too lifted her spirits.

Cole shrugged. "Maybe. I did hear they had an opening on the force."

"It's a great place to live."

Cole glanced at her. "It seems that way, but you wouldn't give up your career to come back here, would you?"

"I could move my practice here. I'd probably have fewer clients, but that's what I need. Mom has always been worried that I'm the only one she has to pass Saltwater Sweets down to. Maybe it's time I stepped up to continue the family legacy."

Cole looked at her, his lips quirking up at the edges. "Soon, she might have a new son to leave it to, though. Me."

Sam laughed. "I'm sure I could use the help."

Cole took her hand, and her heart flipped. "Sounds like we both have some future decisions to make. Maybe we could help each other out by discussing them over dinner tonight?"

"I think that sounds like a great idea."

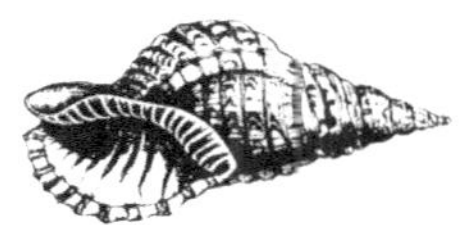

CHAPTER 31

"You can see that thing sparkle all the way over here." Rose pointed her chocolate chip ice-cream cone toward Saltwater Sweets, where Deena was placing a display of chocolate caramel turtles in the window. Her ring glinted in the sunlight.

"It's practically blinding me." Leena crunched into her waffle cone.

"She and Chuck seem very happy now." Pearl dipped her spoon into her kiddie cup and took a tiny bite of vanilla ice cream.

"I know. Isn't it great?" Rose asked. "Even Sam and Cole seem to be on board with it."

"Think we might've had something to do with that, seeing as we helped play up how good Deena and Chuck are for each other," Pearl said.

"Well, it's true, and if we helped them see it, then that was good for everyone." Rose licked around the side of her ice cream so that it wouldn't melt on her hand.

"Good for everyone except maybe Leena. I do appreciate the ice cream, though," Pearl joked.

Leena had lost the bet about whether Deena and Chuck would remain together and as part of that had bought them ice cream.

"Don't worry. Looks like she might get a chance to win another bet." Rose nodded toward the other side of the street, where Sam and Cole were strolling toward Saltwater Sweets hand in hand.

"I feel lucky this time," Leena said. "Those two aren't even from town. It'll never work out."

"I don't know. I heard they were both thinking about staying in Shell Cove now. Cole filled out an application for the local police force." Pearl took another tiny spoonful of ice cream.

"I heard Sam was going to start working at Saltwater Sweets so Deena and Chuck can travel and enjoy their golden years," Rose said.

"We'll see." Leena shoved the rest of the cone in her mouth. "I see someone else might be making some changes too."

Down the street, Gina was staring into the window of the old bakery.

Rose smiled. "Seems like everyone is finding their best future. I think there's going to be a lot of changes in town and all for the better."

❧

Gina peered into the old bakery store and then down at her phone, where her email app was open to the electronic lease for the store and the apartment above.

She hesitated just a second, her finger hovering over the button that would seal the deal. Excitement and nerves warred in her chest.

Hugh had been true to his word and transferred the money into her bank account. She had plenty to cover her first year of business. She had to admit she had felt a pang of sympathy for him when the FBI took him away. It didn't help that he got sentimental and was almost crying as he apologized to her. He said he knew he could always count on her no matter what.

He also asked if she could forgive him for his affair with Holly, and she said maybe. Then he asked if there was a chance they could ever get back together, and she said no way.

She was proud of herself for not wavering. The old Gina would have felt bad for him and crumbled. She would have probably encouraged a reunion. But the new Gina didn't have the slightest desire to do that. Her future was here, and her life with Hugh was well behind her.

She'd wished him the best and sent him off with the fresh baked pie.

Her grandmother had been right. It was much better to enjoy the simple things in life, and that's what Shell Cove had brought her. A simple life and her renewed relationship with her cousins. She'd finally told them the whole story about her split with Hugh, and they'd been very understanding. Unlike what she'd thought, her lie of omission hadn't damaged their friendship.

And now, as she looked into the bakery window, her heart filled with joy. Her mind reeled with ideas for her new venture. She pressed the button and signed the lease.

****

Join my newsletter for sneak peeks of my latest books and release day notifications:

https://lobsterbay1.gr8.com

If you like Hallmark style small town sweet romances, then you're going to love my brand new and very first Christmas Romance - Christmas at Cozy Holly Inn!

USA TODAY BESTSELLING AUTHOR
MEREDITH
SUMMERS
PINECONE FALLS
Christmas
at
COZY HOLLY
INN

ABOUT THE AUTHOR

Meredith Summers writes cozy mysteries as USA Today Bestselling author Leighann Dobbs and crime fiction as L. A. Dobbs.

She spent her childhood summers in Ogunquit Maine and never forgot the soft soothing feeling of the beach. She hopes to share that feeling with you through her books which are all light, feel-good reads.

Join her newsletter for sneak peeks of the latest books and release day notifications:

https://lobsterbay1.gr8.com

This is a work of fiction.

None of it is real. All names, places, and events are products of the author's imagination. Any resemblance to real names, places, or events are purely coincidental, and should not be construed as being real.

SALTWATER SWEETS

Copyright © 2022

Meredith Summers

http://www.meredithsummers.com

All Rights Reserved.

No part of this work may be used or reproduced in any manner, except as allowable under "fair use," without the express written permission of the author.

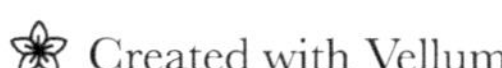 Created with Vellum